DANCING WITH THE DRAGLEON

Guy Waddilove

PEACH PUBLISHING

Front cover image © Glyn Hayes/SL

ISBN 978-1-78036-196-3

Published by
Peach Publishing

Dancing with the Dragleon is dedicated to
TOBIE WADDILOVE,
who may well be disabled, but never stops smiling.
An inspiration to us all and Nathi in particular.

Chapter One

Nisa stood in the doorway of her dark room, peering towards the far corner and the welcome safety of her bed. She held a candle out at arm's length, its weak flame trembling in her hands, casting flickering shadows across the floor.

The monster lived under her bed, but came out at night, Nisa knew.

She'd stayed up as late as she could; dreading this very moment, but it was way past her bedtime now. If only she'd listened to her mum and tidied up her room, but toys, clothes and their shadows littered the floor. The monster could be lying in wait by any of them, right now. Waiting to grab at her bare feet, to snip her and grip her and stab her with its fat, poisoned tail.

By day the monster hid somewhere in the corner, where the cracks in the walls met the floor.

Her father had promised to search for the scorpion, that very afternoon. She'd found just the right stick for him to wheedle it out of its hidey-hole, but he'd been too busy, yet again. The weapon lay ready and waiting for him beside her bed, useless now.

She chewed at her bottom lip, dreading the dash across that floor and the death-defying leap up onto her bed. She had no choice though. The time had come, had passed even.

They could feel your every footstep on the flat scales of their bellies. They could sense your every movement through the bristles on their jointed legs. She could almost feel the monster's many eyes upon her, as it lurked beneath her bed. Or had it come out already? Skulking, somewhere in those shadows on her bedroom floor. The very thought of it made

Nisa shudder.

The candle would be useless once she made a dash for it. She knew from the past few nights how it would flutter and fail, before she ever reached the bed. But reach her bed, she must.

Nisa took a deep breath and blew out the candle, plunging her room into total darkness.

"Now!" she thought, launching into action. With a "Squeak!" she darted across the floor, tip-toeing around things, as fast as her little feet could. She leapt up onto the bed from a distance. It creaked in protest as she landed and scuffled under the covers in one, swift movement.

She'd made it and closed her eyes with a sigh of relief, safe at last. Listening to the lullaby of noises in the night, Nisa could hear her parents in the next room, talking quietly.

"Only a scream away," she thought, calming down as something chirped outside.

"You'll have to do it tomorrow," she heard her mother insist. An owl seemed to agree.

She didn't quite catch her father's reply, thanks to a distant jackal, yipping to its mate.

"Well you'll just have to make time. We can't have her scared of going to bed."

"I know, but that's the third dog that's gone missing in a fortnight," her father hissed, "I have to search for tracks again tomorrow. They're relying on me to help. It's important."

Sinking into sleep began to muffle the sound of their talking, as the cricket chirped again.

"Better the village loses another scrawny dog than we lose our daughter. Besides, she's relying on you too. Which is more important, surely?" she heard her mum say, as a dog barked outside.

"Of course, when you put it like that. I'll do it first thing."

And that was a tree frog.

Nisa heard no more as sleep washed over her in gentle waves, like those that lulled the surface of the local lake, lifting the water lilies and lapping at the reed beds by the shore.

Her father woke her up, early next morning. He pulled aside the flap of skin that covered the only window and fastened it to the wall, flooding her room with welcome light.

"Is this my scorpion stick then?" he asked cheerfully, picking it up and flicking her crumpled clothes to one side of the room, in case it hid under any of them.

No scuttling terror emerged, but Nisa was quick to take advantage of the clear floor. She pulled back the covers, stood up on her bed and leapt as far away from it as she could.

"Thanks Daddy. I know it's there somewhere, probably behind my bed by now."

"Let's see, shall we? Umph," he grunted, hauling her bed away from the walls and into the middle of the room. Its legs raked the hardened earth, leaving drag marks across the floor.

The sudden movement startled their house mantis, which her father said was not a pet. It spread out its spiked arms and turned to watch him with alien, insect eyes.

"Well you're no use!" Nisa cursed it, "Not against scorpions. It's more likely to get you."

The mantis swivelled its head back around to consider her, as if trying to think of an answer. Nisa stuck her tongue out at it, but flinched when it flared out its arms again, in response.

"Sometimes I swear that thing understands more than any insect should," she huffed.

"You leave her alone. I told you, she's a messenger to our ancestors," her dad mumbled.

Nisa stood in the doorway wondering how, exactly? She watched as he got down on hands and knees to inspect the foot of the walls.

"The problem is, that I don't know how high up these cracks go. One of these days, I hope we can build a new house, out of bricks and mortar instead of wood and mud. How would you like that, eh Nisa?" he asked, pushing the stick up into a likely crevice.

She winced and held her breath, expecting a wriggling scorpion to drop down onto his hand.

Nothing. She breathed out again.

He pulled the stick out and tried another crack, able to wiggle it around in this one.

Nisa cringed, but no monster scurried forth, ready to do battle.

She wished her friend the dragleon could help, so named because she looked like a dragon and changed colours, like a chameleon. She didn't act at all dragony either, thank goodness, but there was no way a creature her size could fit in Nisa's room, for all her magical powers and her magical breath and everything. No. They were on their own with this one.

Her father tried each and every nook and cranny, without success.

"It's well and truly holed up in the wall somewhere, I'm afraid. Are you sure this is where it comes out? You've seen it?" he asked.

"I saw it come out from under my bed, is all I know Daddy. It crawled back under there the other morning too. It's going to get me, I know it is," she whined.

"Now Nisa, it isn't out to get you. I told you, it's more scared of you than you are of it."

"Well it must be a real scaredy-cat, then. I hate it being there!"

"It would help if you'd keep your room tidy, like your mother told you to. That way you could see if it's out and about, couldn't you?" her father told her too, "Right, I'm off to see if I can find out what's been happening to the village dogs. There's three gone missing in . . ."

". . . The last fortnight," Nisa interrupted him, "I know. I heard you telling Mummy. Maybe it's the scorpion killing them? While they're sleeping and carrying them off!" her eyes widened.

"Now come on. You know that's not possible. You've seen scorpions. They're only little."

He looked at her like she was just being silly now, which she knew she was, really.

"It takes something much bigger than scorpions and far more dangerous to children, to carry off a dog. So you be careful. You're not to go into the woods on your own at all. Understand?"

Nisa opened her mouth to protest, but thought better of it when she saw how serious he looked. She loved exploring the forest though and finding the dragleon, so they could play together.

"Okay Daddy. I won't. I promise," she hung her head in surly reply.

"Why don't I leave your bed in the middle of the floor? Would that help?" he asked.

Nisa nodded sullenly. It might. Or it might be because he was in a hurry.

The first pitter-patter of rain began outside, marking the end of the long dry season. It sputtered down gently at first, but soon began pounding the ground with round, heavy drops that puffed up wisps of dust wherever they landed.

"That's all I need!" grumbled her father, "We'll never find any tracks now."

Everyone else in the ramshackle village was delighted though, rushing out onto the streets and raising their arms

5

to greet the long-awaited rains. Nisa and her mother laughed out loud as it spattered their bare arms and up-turned, smiling faces.

"We held that Dragleon Festival just in time, eh?" a neighbour, Cecily, called over.

"Only two weeks ago. Perfect timing, I'd say," Nisa's mum replied cheerfully.

Nathi trundled onto the street, beaming up at the skies from his chair with wheels on it. Much as he liked the feeling of warm rain, in time it could make things difficult for him. Mud caked onto the chair's wheels, which he had to turn by hand. Sometimes he got stuck in it too, which really annoyed him. True, his father and any number of grown-ups were only too happy to give him a push, but Nisa knew how he hated having to ask for help, with almost anything it seemed.

"Nisa! Nisa!" squawked his pet grey parrot, from its perch on the back of his chair.

She rushed over to him, the two of them giggling as she spun his chair round and round in the rain. The parrot flapped madly on its spinning perch, screeching in protest.

"It's so nice they get on so well," Nisa's mum remarked.

"Yes. Nathi say his bird really likes her. Taught itself her name, you know?" Cecily replied.

"Oh *you*! Never mind the bird. I meant our children, as well you know," tutted Nisa's mum.

"True. They always played nicely together. Just like us, when we were little, eh?"

"The other children are coming round too, warming to them, from what I hear of school. It's all down to Jasmine, if you ask me. That dragleon's been such a gift to us all, truly."

"I think it's down to your Nisa's sharp tongue. Heh heh! You know what Nathi told me the other day?" Cecily chuckled, "He say that Thabo said his stupid chair always got in the way in class and asked him why he couldn't walk anyway!"

"Oh dear. Mind, Nisa says he can be mean, that one. What did their teacher do about it?"

"She didn't have time to do anything. Heh heh! Because quick as a flash, your Nisa turned round and said 'Because if he could, that would make him more like you! So he'd rather be in his wheelchair!' After that, the teacher was too busy trying not to laugh, Nathi reckoned," and she sputtered out laughing herself, followed by Nisa's mum.

The villagers enjoyed the first downpour of the season, despite the fact there'd be many more. Some would be heavy, some long-lasting and many, no doubt, would be both. By the end of the season they'd all be well and truly sick of rain. Yet for now at least, it lifted everyone's spirits.

"Nisa! Stop that, will you? He's not strapped in, you know," Joseph, Nathi's father called out.

"Oh, sorry," Nathi mumbled, but she stopped laughing and spinning his chair around, much to the dizzy parrot's relief.

"You're supposed to be watching him, Cecily," Joseph reminded his wife, who was still giggling with Nisa's mother. The two of them stood up straight like a pair of naughty schoolgirls, not daring to look at each other.

"Mummy, can I go play with Jasmine in the woods?" Nisa asked, at which Nathi's face fell.

"Of course you can, once it's stopped raining. Mind! You call her from the edge of the forest and wait 'til she comes to get you. You're not to go into the woods on your own at all!"

Nisa scowled at her mum for spoiling her fun.

Nathi cocked his head and wondered why not.

His parrot cocked its head and tried to work out why their mood had changed.

"I mean it, Nisa. Not one step under the trees or anywhere near them, not without Jasmine or a grown-up you know.

Not until your father says it's safe again. Do you hear me?" her mother answered, suddenly turning deadly serious.

"Ooh, good point. We all know what it's like to mean when dogs start going missing," Cecily shuddered gravely, putting a hand on Nathi's shoulder.

Chapter Two

"Jasmine! It's me, Nisa! Are you there?" she hollered from the edge of the woods.

When no reply came she walked around the village clearing, past masses of colourful flowers, which sprang up whenever the dragleon felt happy. They almost surrounded the village by now, since people had taken to feeding her doughnuts, which made the dragleon very happy indeed.

"Jasmine! Can you come here?" Nisa called out, "Because I can't come into the woods to find you. I'm not allowed. None of us are now. So please, if you can hear me . . ."

"Coming! Stay where you are. Be with you in a jiffy," Jasmine yelled back from deep within the woods. The dragleon's hearing was second to none and she could bellow with the best of them, when she wanted to. So Nisa had to wait a while before her enormous friend emerged.

Two shrubs rustled and parted as the dragleon forced her way through, stepping out into the open. They swished back behind her with a flurry of blossom and falling leaves.

Jasmine towered over Nisa, standing before her with open arms and talons.

"What! You're not allowed to give me a hug either?" she demanded, with a smile.

"Of course!" Nisa flung herself into the dragleon's waiting arms and buried her face in the soft, petal scales of her tummy, which changed colour with happiness, "But Daddy says we mustn't go into the woods alone, at all, until he says it's safe again," she explained.

The dragleon stood up, uncurling her long, spiral tail, which she'd been sitting on.

"Why ever not? How will we find each other, if I'm a long way away? I might not hear you calling. And safe from what exactly anyway?" Jasmine fretted.

"I don't know, but it's got something to do with missing dogs. I know that much."

"Oh dear. I hope they're alright, poor things."

"From the way Daddy was talking, I doubt it. He thinks they've been stolen and by something much bigger than scorpions too!" Nisa told her, clambering down from her friend's tummy.

"I wonder if I can help. I'll ask next time I see him, shall I? Come on, we've got some new neighbours I wanted to show you," Jasmine changed the subject. She seemed quite excited, taking hold of the child's hand and leading her to a trail that entered the forest.

All the trees and bushes, grasses and leaves, everything it seemed almost shone green once more, washed clean of its dry season dust at last. The forest itself seemed almost excited, full of different noises, as if coming back to life with the coming of rain. Birds were singing among the branches and calling from the tops of trees. Insects buzzed through the air or chirped where they hid in the bushes. Monkeys shrieked in the distance, from the crowns of nodding palm trees. Everything, everywhere, seemed to be on the move again, bustling and busy. Until the dragleon stopped short and pointed out the busiest, bustling mass of all.

"Look. They come out with the rains. Aren't they amazing? Don't get too close though, will you? They bite," she warned.

Ants, big black ones, were milling up out of a crack in the ground and pouring across the path in a living, endless stream that trickled off into the undergrowth. The sight of them made Nisa's skin prickle, but she couldn't resist bending down for a closer look.

"Wow! I've never seen anything like it. There's so many!" she marvelled.

"They're driver ants. I've seen them before, but not around here. Look at the big soldiers lining the trail, guarding the workers wherever they go. Try breathing on them. Go on, carefully."

Nisa blew out and watched as the trap-jawed soldiers sensed her breath. Instantly they bobbed their fat heads, as one, nipping their jaws together. The movement passed up and down the line in a wave, like an army rattling swords. Within moments, more soldiers had passed on up the line, swelling their ranks right where they sensed her breath, ready to do battle. They raised their heads and clicked their jaws in a rustling rhythm, warning her to keep her distance.

"But how do they know? They can't talk or anything. They can't even see. They've got no eyes, have they? So how do they tell the others to come so quickly, like that?" asked Nisa.

"I've no idea. Maybe they talk in different scents and smells, like we do with different words," Jasmine shrugged, "But they've been teeming up out of the ground for well over an hour now."

"And still they come," Nisa gasped, "Let's follow them, to see where they go."

She stood back up, smiling in wonder as they set off to follow the ants through the undergrowth. The trail soon split in two and split in two again, branching out across the forest floor, which came alive with all manner of fleeing insects. Large and small, they scurried through the dead leaves. Some climbed to the very tips of tall grasses or took flight, trying to get away.

Nisa noticed some ants heading back down the line, carrying bits of dead insects. Several of them sometimes worked together, to lug any larger or longer pieces between

11

them. She wondered how they killed things and asked if they had stingers, like the dreaded scorpion.

"No, I don't think they do. They cover their victims and all hang on like grim death, until they can cut pieces off with their jaws, whilst it's still alive," Jasmine juddered, pulling a face.

"What a horrid way to go!" complained Nisa, secretly hoping she'd see it happen.

"They'll empty the forest of everything that can't get away," Jasmine explained.

The two of them walked along the edge of the column, watching as pieces of plunder got carted back to the nest. There were long spider's legs, chunks of what might've been slugs or snails, bits of beetles and butterfly wings, even other ants. The black, round segments and little red legs of a millipede trundled by, in bits. What looked like the tongue of a big moth, still coiled up in a circle, the head of a big caterpillar, white grubs of some kind or other, still squirming beneath the workers that carried them, all heading back to the nest.

Some columns went up into bushes or up the trunks of trees, all of them searching for prey.

"What's that? Oh no. Look!" cried Nisa, "That's a baby mouse's foot, isn't it?"

"Looks like it," Jasmine agreed, peering into the torrent of ants and spotting the little pink toes, "Anything that can't get away, remember? It doesn't have to be insects or spiders."

"But that's awful! Is that a tail too? Oh those poor baby mice. Can't you stop it?"

"I can't Nisa. It's all part of nature. The ants have to feed and that's sometimes what they feed on, I'm afraid. I'm not sure I could stop so many anyway. They'd just keep on coming."

The chance to prove her point came soon enough, when

Nisa looked up, worried by the cheeping that came from a bird's nest, half way up a tree. Jasmine stood on tip-toes, rearing her long neck to peer into the noisy nest, which was under attack.

"There's only two hatched," she called down to Nisa, "The rest are still safe inside their eggs, thank goodness, but watch this and see what happens."

The dragleon swept her long tail up and down the tree trunk, wiping away any climbing ants. While Nisa watched, more simply veered towards the tree and seethed up towards the nest.

"You see? You can't stop them all."

Young Nisa was determined to try though and snapped a leafy branch off a nearby bush. She hurried back to the tree and brushed away at the ants crawling up its trunk.

The chicks continued twittering in distress, but even more ants poured onto the tree. So Nisa whacked away at them with the leaves, which only maddened them into swarming.

Jasmine looked down at her friend, knowing her efforts would all be in vain.

"OW!" squealed Nisa, suddenly throwing the branch aside and rubbing her hand, "One just bit me! OUCH!" she yelped again, as another ant bit her toe, "That hurt!"

In no time, she was hopping backwards out of the way, clutching at her foot.

"Well you're attacking them, as far as they're concerned. What did you expect? That they'd let you? I did warn you that they bite, these ones," Jasmine answered, lowering herself down.

The hatchlings still cheeped away, up in their nest, while Jasmine tried to comfort her friend.

"It's bleeding. Look. So's my toe!" Nisa complained, sucking at the webbing between her fingers and holding her injured

13

foot with her other hand.

"Try not to blame them. They were only defending themselves," Jasmine explained.

Both of them looked up sadly as the peeping from the nest began to weaken and slow.

When it finally stopped altogether, Nisa began to cry.

"But those poor little chicks and those poor baby mice," she sobbed, "It's horrid. It's not fair."

"I'm afraid not everything in life seems fair, especially when very different lives come clashing together. Sometimes it works out for the best though, eh? Look at us!" Jasmine smiled and carried on, "The ants have babies too, you know? Babies that need feeding and besides, the chicks still inside their eggs will survive. I'm sure the mouse mother will soon give birth again too."

"But won't the horrid ants just get them as well?"

"No they won't. Each day they set off to raid the forest in a different direction. Once they've done a full circle in an area, they all move together to a different part of the forest, where they set up a new nest and start raiding around there instead. I've watched them," Jasmine told her.

"That is clever, in a way," Nisa had to admit, "It's almost like they're farming the forest."

"I suppose so. It allows the forest time to recover, certainly. Things quickly come back home or move on in and don't forget, the ants only come out during the rainy season."

"So?" grumbled Nisa.

"So those chicks yet to hatch from their eggs and any new baby mice will all have grown up and gone, by the time the ants return," Jasmine pointed out.

Nisa looked up and managed a faint smile at that, at least.

"Now I'd better get you safely home, or your parents will be cross with me. Come on."

The two of them set off through the woods, away from the raiding ants. Jasmine figured they'd seen quite enough of life's harsh lessons for one day. Nisa didn't need to see any more.

"It's not a school day tomorrow either, is it?" Jasmine asked.

"No. I used to hate school. The other children were so mean to me because I look different."

"Yes, I remember. They were being perfectly horrid when we first met, but we taught them a lesson or two, didn't we, eh?" the dragleon winked, with a wicked glint in her gentle eyes.

"It's better now. Maybe they learnt their lesson? Mostly they're nicer to me and Nathi too."

"It's about time too. I wish he could come and play in the woods with the rest of you though."

"He'd love to I'm sure, but even the paths are too uneven for his wheelchair," Nisa shrugged.

"He's such a nice boy. It seems a shame. Ah well, tomorrow I'm going for a long walk, beyond my home range. I wondered if you and some of the older children might like to come along."

"That'd be great, like a real adventure. I hope I'm allowed, but I'll have to ask my parents first, at the moment. So will the others, I expect."

"Can you ask your dad if he can bring you to meet me in the morning? I was hoping for a quick word with him about something," the dragleon tried to sound casual, but failed.

"Is it about the missing dogs? Do you know what's doing it? Are you going to scare it away by moving the trees, like you did with that thief? Or breathe on it to make it behave itself, like you did with the monkeys, or make it happy like that snake?" asked Nisa, tugging on Jasmine's talons.

"Steady on and no. I just wanted to ask if I can help. That's all."

"Or you could fight it off, like you did with that big old mean hyena," Nisa got a bit carried away, "Is that what tomorrow's all about? Are we going to look for it?"

"Nothing so horrid, no and not at all. In that order. I want to cheer up the forest a bit further afield, so I've got more living space. Nothing more exciting than that," Jasmine replied.

"Oh well, that still sounds like fun, if I can come," Nisa tried not to look disappointed.

"We'll be going too far for any little ones and you'll need to bring some lunch. So tell your mother, won't you? We'll be alright for drinking water though," Jasmine thought aloud as the forest opened up and they stepped out onto the village clearing, with all its beautiful flowers. The dragleon herself was the only thing that ever looked more colourful, when she was granting a wish. Nisa had seen it only once, watching in wonder as the dragleon's flower petal scales pulsed in waves of every colour she'd ever seen, flashing before her eyes. Just a few of her magical, miracle scales had wafted down to the forest floor and grown into strawberries, for Nisa to eat. And not long after she ate them, she could speak perfectly clearly for the first time in her life and the poor dragleon had to go to sleep. Granting wishes tired her out more than anything, it seemed.

So Nisa had kept it to herself because it wouldn't be fair on Jasmine, who was her best friend, after all. People wouldn't believe her anyway, any more than her parents had, at first. She had to tell them about making a wish with the dragleon, but not what she wished for. That had to stay secret or it might stop coming true and she wouldn't want that and neither would they, she knew.

With a big, happy hug she said goodbye to Jasmine now, but only until tomorrow.

After supper, Nisa found herself standing in the doorway

16

once more, fearful of the scorpion that haunted her room. Her bed still stood in the middle of the floor, where her dad had left it that morning. She could almost leap onto it from here. Almost, but not quite.

"No more staying up 'til all hours. I'm not having it. Now go to bed," he insisted.

Crouching down, she held the candle out at arm's length, to inspect the tidy floor. She had to admit that her mum was right. It was better this way. Not quite so scary now.

As she peered under the bed, a shadow scuttled along the wall. Nisa jumped up, bracing herself, ready to bolt, but soon breathed out with a sigh of relief.

It was only their praying mantis, or rather its shadow in the candlelight, as it climbed up the wall to roost on the clothes hook. It liked it up there.

"Ooh, you wretched thing! You gave me such a fright," she cursed it under her breath and could've sworn it looked back at her, smugly.

"Nisa! I said now!" her father said sternly, somewhere behind her.

She made a dash for it, expecting her foot to be grabbed and stabbed at any moment.

Leaping onto her bed, she dropped the candle on the floor. It rolled, flickered and went out, which worried her. She couldn't reach it from the bed now, if she needed to in the night.

Nisa cowered down under the sheets. She heard nothing but crickets and frogs and maybe a distant hyena, while she drifted off to sleep. A rooster crowed somewhere too, which might've been what woke her up, early the following morning.

Chapter Three

After surviving the night and leaping from her bed, Nisa enjoyed a hearty breakfast and set off with her father. She held on to his hand as half a dozen children joined them, skipping and bouncing along behind. Each of them carried a lunch bag, except Nathi, who wouldn't be with them for long. He spun his wheels to keep up anyway, whilst he still could. Soon they could see the dragleon, waiting for them across the wide clearing. She was hardly small, after all.

The children erupted past Nisa's dad and surged forwards to greet her.

Nathi trundled harder and faster than ever, trying to catch up. His parrot took one look at the monstrous dragleon, thought better of it and fluttered off home without him.

Jasmine swept her arms open wide to scoop up all the giggling children, at once.

As she lifted the whole squirming bunch of them clear of the ground, flowers sprouted all around her, bursting into bloom.

Nisa's dad had to chuckle, watching Nathi hurtle towards them.

"Uh-Oh. Here he comes," the dragleon warned, lowering the children around her and stepping forwards, "Whoa! Little man," she called out, as he flattened the flowers and almost crashed into her. She stuck a foot out to stop his chair and lifted it up at the last minute.

He giggled with glee as she held him aloft and whirled around on the spot. When she plonked him back down, chair and all, the others all cheered, even Nisa's dad.

Jasmine had always had a soft spot for Nathi. So much

so that Nisa teased her about it, saying she must think "such a nice boy" was his surname, but Nisa still felt a bit guilty when he couldn't join them in the woods, even though it was hardly her fault. It was a disease called polio's fault and nobody else's. His mum and dad had told her so, many times, in no uncertain terms.

They said their goodbyes to Nathi and made their way into the woods. While the children tumbled on ahead, the dragleon hung back and tried to speak quietly with Nisa's dad.

"I haven't seen or heard one, but you don't often. They're crafty," Jasmine hissed.

"I know, but please tell us, even if you smell anything," he whispered.

"Yes of course, but do you really think the children might be at risk?" they heard Jasmine ask, at which all the children pricked up their ears.

"Shh," they heard her father hiss, "We don't want to alarm them, but we must be careful."

"Absolutely! I'll keep watch at night, shall I?" Jasmine offered, in a loud whisper.

"I'm sure we'd all sleep more soundly in our beds, if you did. Okay you lot," her father called out, raising his voice as he turned to go, "Have a great time and behave yourselves. Stay close to Jasmine and no playing hide and seek or anything. See you all later. Bye Nisa."

He waved to the children, who all waved back and deeper into the woods they went, bounding around the dragleon and asking endless questions.

"Careful of what? Keep watch for what? Is it dangerous? Is that why we might be at risk? Why should we be alarmed? What don't you often see or hear?" they babbled, all at once.

"Well it can be dangerous to listen in on other people

talking, for a start," snorted Jasmine, "It's called eavesdropping and it's not nice. That's what I'm most alarmed about right now. So you be careful not to do it again, or you might be at risk of being told off, hmm?" she bluffed her way out of answering their barrage of questions.

After a while they came across one of the dragleon's favourite vines. Its pollen was delicious. She asked the children to find the end of it. So they rushed around, tracing its weaving path amongst the trees until they reached the vine's tip, calling her over excitedly.

"Well done!" Jasmine beamed at them, baring her sharp teeth.

She yanked a section of vine free and stretched it out between her clawed hands. With one sharp SNAP she bit right through its woody stem, with no trouble at all. The children gasped.

"There. That should do nicely," the dragleon decided, ramming one end of it into the soft earth and twisting it in deeper, for good measure, "It should sprout roots and grow new shoots in next to no time," she licked her lips and rubbed her tummy, "Seeing as I asked it so nicely."

"If anyone else did that, it would just die," Nisa pointed out.

"Ah, but not for me, and if I like a plant's pollen or nectar, I'd like more of that plant growing in my woods. So I'll have more to eat in future," the dragleon explained, "And things grow back better in the rainy season. So I suppose I'm farming the forest too, a bit like the driver ants do."

"Yes but you're farming plants, not baby mice and birds," Nisa sneered.

"Funny though, it's the other way round for us. We plant our crops at the start of the dry season and harvest them all *before* the rains come. So no chores for us, for a while," a clever girl called Alice shouted out, swinging happily on Jasmine's hand.

As they made their way through the woods, it soon became something of a game. The children looked out for any bushes or vines, which they thought the dragleon might like.

Vines quickly became their favourites because then they could race around, trying to be first to find the vine's tip, which they decided was quite an honour.

"Here's some flowers, Jasmine?" one of the boys yelled back to her.

The dragleon waddled over, walking upright for a while and peering down at the flowers he was pointing at. She wrinkled her snout and pulled back from them.

"What! Are you trying to kill me? I'll have you for that," she joked, grabbing hold of him and tickling his ribs. He begged her to let go, between giggles.

"This one's poisonous. I should know. It's one of mine. Popped up one day when I wasn't very happy. Come to think of it, I was livid, as I recall. This hawk swooped down and snatched up a chameleon that I'd only just been talking to! Poor little thing."

"How can you talk to a chameleon?" one of the girls asked.

"Well, you can talk to just about anything. I never said I expected it to talk back, did I?"

As they came upon a clearing, one of the children turned around, telling the rest to "shush."

A family of warthogs knelt in a line, busily grubbing for grass roots. While two magnificent kudu antelope browsed on a bush, over to one side. Their long horns spiralled up towards the sky, their big ears twitching this way and that. One turned his head to watch them for a moment, before snorting in alarm. In a single graceful bound, both the kudu were gone, while the family of warthogs tottered off into the bushes, with their tails straight up in the air.

Jasmine sighed. It made her so happy to see such lovely creatures in her woods. Clumps of strap-like leaves spread out around her. Flower spikes poked up through them and thrust up higher, bursting open into bright blue balls of delicate bells, like slow motion fireworks.

"Wow!" gasped one of the girls, "They're so pretty."

As they crossed the clearing and came back under the trees, some of the children found a woody vine and pointed it out to the dragleon. It wasn't one of her favourites, but she had an idea for some fun with it, all the same.

"Here, watch this," she told them, clutching the vine in her talons and closing her eyes to concentrate. The children waited, until she let go of it and opened her eyes again.

"Ooh! But that can't be!" gasped Alice.

"It is though. She's moving it, aren't you Jasmine?" asked Nisa, wide-eyed.

"What with? Her mind? But how? That's awesome!" whispered one of the boys.

As the children watched, the vine began to thread itself free of the branches it clung to, unfurling to snake out before them all on its own, weaving slightly, suspended in mid air.

"Can I?" asked Nisa, who couldn't resist reaching out, just to touch that magical moving vine.

Quick as a cobra, its tip curled around and reared up in front of her, as if ready to strike. The vine weaved slowly from side to side, right in front of her face. She jumped backwards, with a squeak! Suddenly unsure, the other children stepped back too, but one of the boys fell over. He landed on his bottom, which made him giggle, nervously. The tip of the vine turned, to 'look' at him instead. Suddenly it shot down towards him, stopping inches from his face, 'daring' him to carry on laughing. He stopped laughing alright, when his jaw dropped open.

Jasmine couldn't help giggling, which broke her concentration. The vine flopped harmlessly to the forest floor, before rising back up to twine through the branches and twigs once more.

"You should always put things back where you found them," she announced. Twirling her talons to direct the twisting vine, she smiled at the wonder on their up-turned faces.

"Whoa! How did you learn to do that?"

"That's some trick, Jasmine. It's amazing! Moving things, without even touching them!"

"Glad you liked it, but it's not really that difficult, once you know how. You have to sort of remember what the plant feels like and think that bit harder, but I'm not very good at it yet."

"Oh, yes you are! That was fantastic!"

"Oh, no I'm not!" "Oh, yes you are!" "Oh, no I'm not!" and so it continued, for some time.

As they wandered deeper into the woods, the children begged her to repeat the trick. She would have and gladly, only now she remembered how drained it left her feeling.

"Look! Footprints in the sand," one of the girls pointed out, "I wonder what made them?"

"Looks like a big dog to me, kind of," one of the boys decided, "Do you know, Nisa?"

"No it's not a dog because there's no claw marks on the end of the toes," she worked out.

"And not hyena because the back feet are as big as the front feet. So it must be a big cat, like a leopard," Nisa gulped and looked up at Jasmine, because all of a sudden, everything made sense.

Leopards worried the dragleon. They weren't the most dangerous animals in the forest, not to her, but they were so good at hiding and so fast. If ever one did strike, at your face

23

from a branch or out from under your feet, you never saw it coming, so it always came as something of a shock. Quite suddenly, she all but disappeared, blending in perfectly with the plants around her. Her scales took on their colour and texture, until all you could make out were her big, gentle eyes.

"Oh Jasmine!" the children complained, "Do you have to do that?"

"We can't see you when you do your disappearing trick. We might bump into you."

"Nisa's dad said 'no hide and seek', remember? So that's not fair."

They had a point and as if by magic, the dragleon reappeared, right before their eyes.

"Sorry. I'm afraid I do it without thinking sometimes, if something makes me nervous," she admitted, "Like having to look after you lot when there's a leopard on the prowl. There aren't any other paths for a while either. So we're stuck on this one, for the time being."

Nisa led the way. Like her father and his father before him, she had a talent for tracking. She read the broken trail like a book, even working out which way the cat had gone, when its prints ran out for a while. It seemed amazing to the others, how she could tell where it stopped or crouched down, had jumped a log or brushed through a clump of grass on its way.

"Ooh, Nisa. I'm getting scared, if it's a leopard an' all," one of the boys whimpered.

"And you called me a 'cry baby' once. Remember?" she taunted him.

"And I want to go potty in the bushes, but I daren't if there's a leopard," Alice declared.

A nice girl who liked dolls, Nisa had noted, poor Alice seemed almost beside herself.

Although whether it was down to the leopard or needing

the toilet, Jasmine wasn't sure.

"Oh good. At last! Here's another path. Let's go that way," she pointed down another trail.

They carried on through Jasmine's rich forest for a while, walking around great baobab trunks, dodging thorny acacia trees, pushing their way past thick, wet bushes and wading through wafting green grasses, shaded by a sunlit tapestry of leaves and palm fronds, high above their heads.

They reached a freshly flowing stream, dry for some time before the rains began, but already trickling down towards the river once more.

The far side of its shallow gulley looked parched and sandy. Scrawny fawn grasses grew fewer and brittle beige bushes grew farther apart. Even the trees looked spindly and somehow grey. Some impala antelope eyed them nervously in the distance. They bounded off, leaping every which way, leaving puffs of dust to billow up behind them as they disappeared.

Even the children couldn't fail to notice the difference between the two sides of the stream.

"Right. We've reached the edge of my home range now," the dragleon stated the obvious.

"Is that what it used to look like before you came, Jasmine?" one of the boys asked.

"Nearer the river it never got so dry, but this far from it, yes," she told them.

They walked along the lush bank of the gulley, while Jasmine eyed the plants on the far side.

Nisa was watching where she put her bare feet, as usual. She'd been following some tiny tracks in the sandy soil, wondering what could have such teeny-weeny hooves. She began to worry for whatever it was, when the leopard's paw prints appeared along this trail too.

"Jasmine!" she hissed, "The leopard's back. Look."

"We'd better go a different way then. Ooh, leopards! And this one seems determined to spoil our fun, doesn't it?" Jasmine complained, as the scales that ran down her back turned thorny.

"It went that way, in through those bushes," Nisa pointed out.

"Ooh, look. The other way. Ha ha! Perfect. That's a marula tree. My favourite! Come on."

The dragleon waddled directly over the stream and away from the leopard tracks. The children followed eagerly, especially poor Alice, who'd been hopping from one foot to the other, whilst they'd all been standing still.

Everyone liked marula fruit. Jasmine reached up to pick what fruits were left and handed some to the children. The rest she ate herself, rolling them around in her mouth to savour. She spat the stones out, one by one, whilst turning around in a slow semi-circle.

"Sorry everyone. Not a very grown up thing to do, I know, but a very good way to plant the pips, all the same," she excused herself.

To her horror, the children all copied her, turning round slowly as they spat the pips out.

"Now don't you go telling your parents or worse, actually doing that in front of them, will you?" she worried, "Or they'll think I'm teaching you some very bad manners, when I'd never."

"You just did though," one of the boys answered her back. Rather cheekily, she thought.

"Ooh, you wouldn't get me into trouble, like that," Jasmine scoffed. At least, she hoped not.

As they wandered through the dry scrub and away from the prowling leopard, Alice plucked up the courage to go to the toilet behind a bush, much to everyone's relief, but especially hers.

The dragleon gathered seed pods to scatter in the dust. She had to stamp on some to open them up, which the children were only too happy to help her with. She searched out shrubs that she liked to eat, breaking off the odd branch to plant in the sandy soil, as only she could get away with.

When they found a second stream the children sat down to eat their lunches. At the bottom of Nisa's bag was a large packet, stuffed full of doughnuts, on which her mum had written "one each" in large letters. Nisa began to hand them out, one at a time. Everyone loved her mum's doughnuts. A line of drool slipped out between the dragleon's sharp teeth, to slop upon the sand. Nisa pretended to scrunch the paper bag up and burst out laughing at the sad look on her face.

"And yes, of course. You know my mum, Jasmine. There's a huge one here, just for you!"

She handed her friend one enormous doughnut, which looked more like a loaf of bread!

As the dragleon bit into it, the brittle bushes all around them burst back into life, first budding and then bursting into leaf once more. Green shoots poked up from long dormant seeds in the ground, sprouting into clumps of grass or bunches of pretty wild flowers.

After lunch they carried on through the dry scrub, chasing after mongooses, just for fun, replanting this, clearing that, sowing these seeds and scattering those.

They headed in a wide arc, back to the stream that marked the edge of Jasmine's home range, where Nisa noticed a cloud of flies buzzing around a tree, which seemed odd. She went to have a look, swatting away at the pesky flies as she pushed through the bushes by the tree's base.

Suddenly Jasmine's head shot up, scenting the air deeply.

"Nisa don't!" the dragleon called out, too late.

"Oh dear. Oh Jasmine, look what it's done," Nisa almost whispered.

A slender body lay draped over a fork in the tree, still dripping, its bare teeth exposed in a lifeless grin. Most of its insides had gone and there wasn't much left of its back legs either.

It was a dainty dik-dik antelope and judging by its pencil thin front legs, no doubt the owner of those tiny hooves, which Nisa had been tracking earlier. She stepped backwards through the bushes, unable to take her eyes off it. Seeing such a pretty creature, all dead and mangled like that, seemed so very wrong to a small girl.

Jasmine herded them all away, thinking she could smell toffee popcorn. She knew the leopard would not have gone far. It was probably watching them, right now. At the very thought of it studying the children, her scales turned all thorny. They set off home straight away.

Nisa noticed that Jasmine seemed very quiet on the way back. She kept looking over her shoulder, or stopping to sniff the air, as if making sure they weren't being followed.

Worried for the children in her charge, the dragleon led them straight back home, no longer stopping to prune this or sow that, or practice any of her magical powers over plants.

The route took them by where they'd watched the driver ants, only the day before. The woods round about seemed eerily quiet, but there was no other sign that the ants had ever been there. Sure enough, having cleared this part of the forest, they'd moved on to pastures new.

Chapter Four

Nathi had been watching out for her, when Nisa returned to tell him of the day's adventures. They went to give the two donkeys a fuss, as Nisa often did on her way home.

His parrot hopped onto her shoulder and rubbed the top of his head on her cheek.

"He really likes you. He never does that to anyone, but me," Nathi congratulated her.

"I don't want him making a habit of it. I don't really trust him and I don't want him pooing down the back of my dress either. Mum would kill me," she answered nervously, but didn't dare shoo the parrot off, in case it bit her or did something worse, which might ruin her dress.

"He wouldn't, Nisa! He's very well behaved. I trained him myself," Nathi protested.

"That's what I'm worried about," she teased him.

"Nisa! Nisa!" the parrot squawked in her ear, bobbing up and down and nearly deafening her.

"Oh no. Not this again. Can't you get him to screech something else?" she begged.

"Nisa! Nisa! Nathi! Nathi!"

"Ooh! He just did!" the two of them looked at each other and started laughing.

Next she told her mum what they'd been up to all day, before trudging into her room . . .

. . . And bursting right back out of it!

"Mummy! Mummy! There's another mantis attacking ours! Quick! What do we do?"

When her mum didn't seem at all worried, Nisa rushed back into her room, confused.

29

"Oh it's alright. She's winning!" she called out, "Because she's bitten its head off now and she's eating it! Vile thing. Oh no! They're still attached though, from when they were fighting!"

"She'll be fine, Nisa. Leave them be. Come back in here and show me what those tiny hoof prints looked like, why don't you?" her mother managed, trying not to laugh.

When Nisa came back into the room, she could tell her mum had been sniggering. She was trying hard not to now. Nisa had no idea what could be so funny, but suspected it had something to do with the mantis fight, which didn't seem funny at all.

"Daddy wouldn't think it was funny! He would've saved her," she blurted out.

"Oh I'm sure he would," her mother replied, with a definite titter.

"Would what? Have thought it was funny? Or tried to save her?" demanded Nisa.

Her mother could no longer contain herself and burst out laughing, once and for all.

Nisa scowled at her, which only made matters worse. Her mother laughed all the harder for it anyway. So Nisa stormed outside to stomp around the village for a while. When rain clouds rolled on in to drench what remained of the day, she took shelter under a shop porch.

She became aware of the owner. He was watching her every move through the window, staring at her like their house mantis did, which gave her the creeps. His was a general store, selling tools and home ware with a few toys in amongst, hanging up or stacked in neat piles all around her.

Being half Bushman, Nisa already knew what people often thought of "her sort", as she hated being called. At markets certainly, she'd often been thought of as a little thief, but not here in her own village, not any more, where people ought to know better by now, surely. He carried on staring at her though, as if fully expecting her to steal something.

She never had and never would either. Her father would kill her for a start and he was, well, whole Bushman! She wondered which half of her was Bushman anyway; her top half, or the bottom half? Her left half, or the right? She also wondered why people said "your sort" instead of just saying Bushman. Nisa reckoned it said far more about the person saying "your sort" than it ever did about her. Often they were unkind and unfair and all too often, towards her!

Still, he hadn't said anything of the sort yet. He might just be wary of everyone. Nisa being Nisa decided to find out, peering very closely at this or that, humming with her hands behind her back. The man inside shifted uneasily, she noted.

Picking up a large box with a doll inside it, she turned it around in her little hands and sure enough, the shop keeper suddenly appeared in the doorway, with his arms folded.

"How much is this, please?" she asked politely, having no interest in dolls whatsoever.

"Do you have any money on you?" he scowled down at her.

"Not at the moment, but I might come back with some, if I can afford it?"

"Then I'll be sure to keep it indoors from now on, where I can keep an eye on it," he growled.

"Oh. To save it for me? Thank you." She smiled up at him.

"No. To save it from you. Now be off with you. Go on!"

"But it's still raining and hard," Nisa protested.

"I don't care. Put the doll down. I'll give you 'not at the moment'. Not ever, more like! You don't fool me. You've no intention of paying for it. Your sort never does."

He may as well have slapped her in the face. Nisa stiffened as if he had.

31

The shop keeper leaned forwards and snatched the box back off her! It broke open and the brand new doll slid out, as if in slow motion, to land on the damp dirt floor.

"Look what you made me do! You'll pay for that! I can't sell it now. It's dirty," he shouted. "You did that on purpose, you little thief!" he ranted on until she butted in, to correct him.

"I didn't make you do anything. Your own thinking bad of my 'sort' of people made you do that and the word is Bushman, by the way. Or San, if you prefer, but never 'your sort!'"

The shop keeper looked taken aback as Nisa carried on. She hadn't quite finished yet.

"I won't pay for it either, but you will because you're right. Her dress is all dirty, so you can't sell it now and it serves you right for thinking me a thief, when I never have and I never would either! And I'm glad it's cost you, ooh, whatever that doll cost you. Maybe that'll learn you a lesson!" Nisa ranted right back at him and sped off into the pouring rain, before he could reply.

"Teach," he said to her back as she disappeared, "Teach me a lesson. Not 'learn.'"

His brain mulled over what had just happened. The worst of it was the nagging feeling that she was quite right. He had thought the worst of her, because of her sort. So maybe it was his fault? How would he like being called a thief, when he wasn't? He felt a little ashamed, if still slightly confused, but he'd never thought about stuff like this before, when maybe he should have. He would right now, he decided. So maybe she had 'learned' him a lesson after all. He went inside, thinking he might just give her the doll the next time he saw her, by way of an apology.

The rain forced Nisa back indoors, soaking wet. She told her about the shop keeper, but her mum just told her to change into some dry clothes. At least she'd stopped laughing at her now.

Their mantis had definitely won her gruesome battle, having eaten the rest of her attacker by suppertime, while Nisa watched. She felt so hungry, she could've eaten it herself!

Afterwards she dashed across her room and onto her bed again, because it was getting dark.

Nisa must've drifted off to sleep, because something woke her in the dead of night. The rain had stopped, but she didn't think that was it. She listened, waking up while she worked it out.

Dogs! It was dogs. They were going mad out there, not far down the lane either.

Still half asleep, Nisa reached down for the candle beside her bed.

The scorpion twirled around, to face the sudden threat.

Her hand tapped lightly around the floor.

While the scorpion danced out of the way.

She heard the tell-tale rattle of the matchbox and grasped for it in the darkness.

The scorpion flared its pincers, threatening her fingers.

Having picked up the matches, Nisa reached back down to find the candle.

The scorpion quickly dodged her hand, raising its tail, ready to strike.

She groped around, forcing the scorpion to back away, jerking its tail as a final warning, until it straddled the very candle she was feeling for. As her fingers found and gripped the smooth shaft, the scorpion had finally had enough. Nisa picked it up, as the scorpion struck! Its tail whipped forward to sting her hand, just as it slipped from the smooth wax and fell to the floor.

As she struck a match to light the candle, the scorpion

scuttled back to its hidey-hole. Only then did Nisa think to inspect the floor, to make sure it wasn't there.

She would never know how close she'd come, to being stung to death.

She got out of bed and lifted the flap of skin that acted as a curtain. Peering out of her window proved useless. It was pitch black out there. She could hear the dogs going crazy though, yipping and snarling at something. When she held the candle out against the darkness, she could see them worrying at some small, hapless creature, trapped and terrified against the base of a wall.

"Poor thing," she whispered and clambered through her window, out into the night.

The dogs turned to face her as she approached, holding the candle out in front of her.

"Shoo! Go on, get away!" she hissed, scattering them behind her, with their tails up.

Further up the street, two pin pricks of light closed briefly, as the prowling leopard blinked.

Nisa bent down to see what the dogs had been tormenting. It was a harmless house snake. They were useful, keeping dangerous snakes away from the home. They ate them, her dad said.

This gave the leopard choices it hadn't been expecting. Another dog? Or the human child? It was bigger than the dogs, but he hadn't hunted humans before. Whereas he knew what he was doing with dogs. They were easy. The human stood up and turned around, holding a long, dark snake in her hands. It confused the leopard for a moment. He wouldn't risk that. Instead he crouched down to watch and listen, unseen and unheard by the dogs, or Nisa.

She struggled to keep the snake away from the candle flame on her way back to the window.

Once there, she found she had a problem, getting herself, the snake and the candle inside?

All the while the leopard watched her and the wound-up dogs, weighing up its options.

Nisa dropped the snake in through the window and clambered in after it. Luckily she thought to turn around and fasten the curtain back to its peg on the wall.

The dogs drifted off, their fun here over now, but the leopard knew they'd be wide awake and on the alert for a good while yet, so best leave them be tonight.

Nisa picked up the snake and put it in a wicker basket, as the leopard stole up to her window, silently. It reared up to sniff at the flimsy covering of skin. She placed the lid back on the basket, while the leopard listened to her movements inside. That strange, flickering light unnerved him though. So he thought better of it and melted back into the night, to hunt something else.

It was something much bigger than scorpions and far more dangerous to children that her little candle had saved her from, that night.

"Nisa. Get up, will you?" her mother told her, "It's long past sun up. Your dad's already out with some of the men, having a look round," she mentioned brightly, picking up this and tidying that in Nisa's room, "Whatever's the matter with you this morning, Sleepyhead?" she wanted to know as she went to put some clothes in the laundry basket.

"AAAARGH!" she screamed, slamming the lid back down on the basket.

Nisa sat bolt upright in her bed "Whoa, wha, what's 'at?"

"Snake!" her mother screeched, "In the laundry basket! Quick! Get a shovel, Child."

"Eh? Oh. It's alright Mummy. It's a house snake. He's harmless, friendly even. I rescued him."

"Oh Nisa, for goodness sakes! You nearly had to rescue me, from a heart attack!"

"But he'll keep all the bad snakes away. He'll eat them. It's what they do. Can't I keep him?"

Bleary-eyed, she plodded over and took the lid off the laundry basket. To her mother's horror, she reached inside and lifted the snake out; squirming around her hands and up her arms, but making no move to strike her at all, her mother had to admit.

"See?" Nisa held him up to show her how sweet he was, really.

Her mum was not entirely convinced, leaning back and pulling a face.

"We-ell, I suppose they are good at keeping snakes and rats away too, but mind you keep it out from under my feet, do you hear? I'll have a word with your father and see what he thinks. He knows about this sort of thing," she granted, against all her better instincts.

Her father stalked through the streets ahead of a group of men, including some of the elders.

Every so often he stooped to the ground, touching it or stroking it softly, as if trying to make sense of the slightest signs. He was tracking. With the ground softer after the rain, they'd found the odd paw print. It seemed almost supernatural to the others, how on earth he could tell which way the leopard had gone. Even when it jumped up onto a roof, he guessed where it would come back down, from this building or the next. It made no difference. Somehow he just knew, but there was no longer any doubt as to what had taken

36

the village dogs. Or last night's goat either.

"He rushed forward here," he worked out, raising his head to follow the trail down the street, "Oh no!" he gasped and hurried down the lane. With his heart pounding in his chest, he stopped short and swallowed hard, staring in shock at the wall of his own hut and the ground beneath it.

"He stood up on his hind legs, right here," he gulped, "To look through my Nisa's window," he said to no-one in particular and sank to his knees, suddenly feeling sick.

Two men helped him back up onto his feet. He looked down at the ground again. His eyes widened as his gaze led further down the street. It had even stopped to sniff at her little footprints.

"NISA!" he bellowed suddenly, "Get out here, RIGHT NOW!" he roared.

It shocked those around him. One of the elders clutched at his own chest.

Nisa dropped a spoon inside the hut, while her mother looked up in surprise.

"I said NOW!" her father shouted.

Nisa rushed outside trembling, to be greeted by half the village, it seemed.

"What Daddy?"

"I'll give you 'what!' LOOK! Here! What's this, eh?" he screamed at her, grabbing hold of the back of her neck and forcing her head down to look at the dirt, "You STUpid, STUpid child!"

Nisa burst into tears, wailing as her father held her face down in an angry, vice-like grip.

"Steady on. That's enough now, surely," one of the elders tried to step in on Nisa's behalf.

Her father was having none of it though, despite his daughter's pleas for mercy. Disgusted, he threw her face down into the dirt and stormed off in a rage.

"What on earth?" her mother gasped, as she came round the side of the hut.

"A goat was taken last night and we were tracking what took it," one of the elders explained.

"Right to young Nisa's window, I'm afraid. It seems she took it upon herself to go for a walk at some point in the night and very nearly got taken herself. Look. See for yourself."

"Oh Nisa. Rescuing that stupid snake, yes?" her mother guessed, kneeling down to pick her up, "From what, a leopard! What were you thinking of?" her mother hugged her, rocking slowly back and forth, "No wonder your father's so upset. You could've been killed!"

"From the dogs," Nisa mumbled, wiping her snotty nose with the back of her arm, "They were attacking it. It's only a few yards," she managed between sobs, "Down the . . ."

"Never mind excuses, Nisa. You were nearly killed!" her mother butted in, "Look at me," she growled, holding her daughter's cheeks in the palms of her hands and staring into her eyes, "Now, do you admit that leaving your room at night, without telling either of us, was a very silly thing to do, thoughtless and dangerous even, especially at the moment?"

Nisa felt so stupid she could hardly speak. Never in her life had she been so embarrassed. She could only lower her eyes and nod her head, in shame.

"Make no mistake; I am so cross with you right now," her mum almost snarled at her.

Nisa started to cry all over again, when she noticed Nathi staring at her from his front door.

"Tears won't help either. Just go to your room and stay there, while I go and discuss what to do with you, with your father. And he has every right to be so angry with you. Do you understand?"

"Yes Mummy. I'm really sorry. Tell Daddy I'm sorry too," she mumbled.

Chapter Five

As the dragleon stepped out from the forest, she spotted Nisa's dad. He was sitting alone on a log, with his elbows on his knees and his face buried in his hands. It seemed so unlike him.

Dropping down onto all fours, Jasmine walked up to him, with her tail coiled up and her ears drooping. Ever so gently, she asked him what could be so wrong.

He told her about the prowling leopard, stalking his beloved Nisa in the night.

"It did WHAT!" raged the dragleon, instantly flashing black and blood red, before cocking her head to one side and fading to orange and burnt yellow, "But how?"

He told her about Nisa, clambering out of her bedroom window in the dead of night.

"She did WHAT!" howled the dragleon, suddenly burning orange again, "But why?"

"I'm ashamed to admit I don't know. I was so angry, I didn't stop to ask," mumbled Nisa's dad. He went on to tell her how he knew he'd been too rough on her.

"You did WHAT!" exclaimed the dragleon, fading back to a confused yellow. For when he looked up at her with tears in his eyes, Jasmine found that she couldn't stay cross with him. She decided to be absolutely livid with the leopard instead.

"RIGHT! We'll soon see about THAT!" she snarled and stomped off towards the village, working herself up into a giant, spiky rage! She was angry with Nisa and Nisa's dad, but most of all, she was furious with that leopard! Her scales seethed from jet black to blood red, flashing orange with bursts of yellow and back to red and black again. The dragleon may not be able to breathe fire, but it looked like she'd burst into flames herself, as she blazed across that clearing.

Nisa's father stood up, looking concerned. He called after the dragleon, but it was no use. The dragleon was in no mood to listen right now, muttering away to herself.

"Soon put a stop to THAT! I'm not HAVing it!" she rumbled, not even stopping when she passed Nisa's mother, who was heading in the opposite direction. She turned slowly to watch the dragleon marching off in the monster of all huffs, wondering if Nisa had caused her thunderous temper and whether or not she should follow.

Jasmine stamped around the village like an earthquake, ignoring everyone. The ground shook.

"How DARE it! Not my Nisa. Oh no. NEVER again!" she snarled away to herself. CRASH! BANG! WALLOP! Round and round she stomped, growling in a fit of rage.

People stopped what they were doing, standing open mouthed as they watched her surge past.

The first thorn bush burst up from the ground. It ripped up through the red soil and began to spread. More and more erupted out of the ground in the dragleon's wake.

Before long they surrounded the village, their branches spearing out to meet their neighbours.

Jasmine stopped and stood before the ring of thorns. Her eyes blazed, her scales as sharp as the thorns themselves. Breathing in deeply, she flung her arms open wide, wafting and waving them about. She twirled her talons, tracing circles, figures of eight and slashes in the air, like a conductor leading an orchestra, made of vicious thorns. The bushes obeyed her every whim, following her gestures and furious movements, their branches stretching, twisting and turning, weaving and tangling, bending and seething, until they'd scraped and scratched together, interlocking to form a thick, ferocious barrier that no leopard, however determined, would ever be able to cross.

She stamped further around the ring of thorns, repeating the process all over again, and again, until finally satisfied that nothing would find the slightest chink, to slip or slither through.

"Without getting torn to SHREDS!" she sneered, wiping her hands together in triumph.

"Job well done, I think," she reckoned, beginning to feel happier again.

She had indeed, done a very thorough job, one of the elders decided. He stood open-mouthed before the wall of thorns, which barred his way up the main road and out of the village.

A fishermen scratched his head on the river road, wondering how he was supposed to get back to his hut, which stood inside the towering thorns.

"Whose darned silly idea was this?" he shouted, to anyone listening.

Nisa's mother and father rushed up to join Jasmine.

"Um. Hello. Is anybody there?" the elder called out, feebly, "Only, I'd like to be, you see?"

"And I need to get to the school, quick sticks! If you'd be so kind," the teacher added, primly.

"Ah. Yes. I hadn't thought of that," mumbled the dragleon, turning a lovely shade of pink.

"Evidently!" complained Gloria, the teacher, "But I do have lessons to prepare, you know?"

Jasmine looked over her shoulder to where the school building sat, outside the protective thorns. Clearly, the teacher had a very good point.

"Ahem! And we'd like to get back in, Jasmine," Nisa's mum pointed out, pointedly.

"To tell our daughter what her punishment will be. She'll

be expecting us, I'm sure. In fact I hope she's dreading our return, but return we must!" her dad added.

"OI! What's this? How am I supposed to get to my storage shed?" Some of which also stood outside the thorns, Jasmine realised.

"Who the blazers put that there? Me goats is outside, on their own now."

"It wasn't there a while ago. Mind, I suppose I could hang my laundry on it. Certainly won't blow away. Oh, but it might get holes in it. OW! They're sharp," a washerwoman babbled inside.

"It's right around the village!"

"We're trapped in here, we are."

"Plenty of firewood for the ovens now though, eh?" somebody reckoned, raising a hatchet.

The sound of someone chopping wood made the dragleon wince. She heard a faint rustle.

"Oh. Perhaps not. Will you look at that! Soon as you chop a bit off, it grows it back double."

"Well stop chopping it then, before the whole village is smothered in thorns. Silly fool!"

"Hey! Someone let us out, will you?"

"I presume this was your doing, Jasmine?" Joseph yelled from inside, "Might I suggest some doors or gateways, or something? I'll make them, if you could provide the gaps?"

"Ooh, I'm ever so sorry everyone," gushed the dragleon, having turned as pink as pink can be, "I'm afraid I was so cross, I didn't stop to think, beyond protecting the children against that leopard. It hunted poor Nisa last night, you know?"

"Not nearly as well as it hunted one of my goats!" the goatherd griped, "The rest of which will be wandering off to who knows where, as we speak!"

"Well, you'd better think of something now. And be quick

43

about it!" the teacher snapped.

"Here, Here!" agreed the elder.

"Right. Of course. Um, err," the dragleon sounded flustered.

"Jasmine! Are you there? Because I'm standing on the main road now, right where we need to clear some of these blasted thorns of yours! I haven't got all day," the elder told her, flatly.

"Of course I'm here and there's no need to shout. I get it. I get it, alright? Hold on."

The dragleon laid her talons on one of the wicked thorn bushes, as tall as a tree. It flopped harmlessly to the floor like a pile of black spaghetti.

She grinned at the elder, the goatherd and the teacher, waiting impatiently on the other side. They carried on about their business, with the elder muttering away to himself about having something else to discuss at the next village meeting now, he supposed.

"And maybe this one too, I think," Joseph decided, "To widen the gap, for carts and such."

The dragleon laid her talons on the next bush along and again, it wilted and drooped into a pile of harmless, squiggly strands. She made her way to the two other main paths out of town, or at least they would be, once she'd cleared them of brutal thorn bushes. She walked through the village, keeping her head down. Some people seemed to like the new thorn fence, while others were shaking their heads at her. Whatever they thought of it though, the village now boasted its very own leopard proof fence.

Joseph set out straight away to find suitable tree trunks, to act as massive gateposts.

Nisa cowered in her room, awaiting her punishment, whatever that might be.

Her father had calmed down eventually. In truth, he was more upset than angry, but the two so often go hand in hand with parents, when their children put themselves in danger.

Even so, Nisa had to do a heck of a lot of chores over the next few days and was well and truly grounded, banned from going into the forest at all, with anyone, until further notice.

By the fourth day she was well and truly fed up, bored and missing her dragleon friend.

Nathi did his best to keep her company, when she wasn't busy with extra chores. He'd been told off himself though, for helping her when he shouldn't have, because she was being punished.

"She'll never learn to do as she's told or think before she acts, not if you make the lesson any easier for her," his father had explained, between bouts of hammering gateposts into the ground and cursing awkward roots and vicious, fiddly thorns.

Nisa was complaining bitterly to Nathi as they sat together on the jetty, down by the river.

"It's do this and do that and when you've finished, go and help so and so with such and such because he or she's so old. Daddy even boarded my window up. Can you believe that?"

But mostly she was moaning about not being able to play with Jasmine, out into the woods.

"Nisa, you do know that all this is meant to teach you to think, before you act?" Nathi asked.

"Oh yes. How many times have I heard that, over the last few days?"

"Well it's not working very well then, is it? Because sometimes maybe, you should think before you say something too. Saying something's an act in a way, isn't it?"

"Yes I suppose, but what're you getting at?" Nisa answered impatiently. Her mood soon softened though, when she noticed his bottom lip trembling. Was he crying?

"Well what do you think it's like for me?" he suddenly

blurted out, but Nathi never cried!

"Because I can never go and play in the woods with Jasmine, or the rest of you. How can I? When I'd like to more than anything else in the whole, wide world! But it doesn't do to complain about it, not for me. Oh no, because it won't change anything, will it? I still won't be able to go. Not ever! Not in this stupid chair! So please stop moaning just because you can't go for a few days. How do you think that makes me feel?" he started sobbing, face down in his folded arms.

Nisa was horrified; to think she might've upset him. She was almost in tears herself.

"Oh Nathi. I'm so sorry. I didn't mean to, I didn't think and you're right. I should have, but you've just taught me better than any amount of chores ever would. Right here and now."

"And don't you go telling my mum that I got upset on it either. I'm not allowed. Not ever! Or yours, because she'll only tell mine and I'll still get told off," he sniffled, looking up.

"I won't. I wouldn't, I promise."

"Good!" he recovered, snuffling as he wiped the tears from his round, wet cheeks.

They sat together in silence for a while, watching some fishermen on the river banks, twisting and turning with their fishing rods to swish their long lines back and forth.

"Tell you what I could do though. Don't see why not. They're not using their legs much," Nathi thought aloud. A big, broad smile spread across his face, where one seemed to belong.

"What? Tell me! Can I help?" Nisa almost shook him.

"Yes, you can, by asking the fishermen if one of them can lend me a rod, so I can have a go."

Nisa smiled and shook her head slowly. Nathi never ceased to amaze her.

46

That was the first time she'd ever heard him complain about being in a wheelchair, let alone seen him upset about it. Yet he'd recovered so quickly, with the idea of something that he could do, replacing any thoughts of what he couldn't.

Since it was her who'd upset him, she really wanted to help. She'd hardly ever heard him ask for help before either, come to think of it. So it felt like an honour to be asking one fisherman after another, if any of them had a spare rod she could borrow, for Nathi to practice with.

Eventually one of them looked over to where he was sitting and seemed to take pity on him. He offered her a partly snapped rod and some line to go and play with. It was the best they were going to get, she figured. So she accepted it gratefully and took it back to Nathi.

He tied the line to the hook and threaded it through the small hoops on the rod, as he'd seen the fishermen doing, or so he thought. It was kind of hard to tell from this distance.

"Alright, here goes," he cast the line behind him, ready to flick it forwards into the river.

There was a pathetic little tinkle and the nearest men started sniggering.

"Hang on Nathi," Nisa gave the fishermen a filthy look as she got up to find the hook.

Some of them gathered round to watch. This might get entertaining, after all.

"Here it is!" she called, bringing the hook back, "You can't have tied it on properly."

"Better luck next time, eh?" one of the men called out, which the others seemed to find funny.

"Mind your fingers there, Boy!" yelled another fisherman, while Nathi threaded the hook.

He tried again, but this time the hook got caught between the wooden slats of the jetty and nearly yanked his arm off when he went to cast the line forwards. He dropped the rod behind him.

The fishermen burst out laughing, some of them slapping their thighs and pointing.

Nisa freed the hook and brought it back, suggesting he cast to one side and not backwards.

This time he narrowly missed his parrot, which had to duck where it perched on his chair.

"You're supposed to be fishing, not parroting!" one of the men joked, to howls of laughter.

Nathi tried again. The hook got caught on a root, sticking up out of the river bank.

"Look! He caught himself a bush! Fight it, Boy!" which had them laughing their heads off.

He tried again. The hook stuck in the ground and Nisa freed it for him, to gales of laughter.

"It's no use. I'm not high up enough," he hissed, refusing to admit defeat.

Nathi hauled himself awkwardly back down the jetty, plank by plank, using only his arms. His wasted legs trailed behind him, the toes of his shoes clattering against the wood. He pulled himself up and into his chair, turning round to sit down in one, heavy movement.

Most of the fishermen stopped laughing, their smiles draining from their faces.

Nisa followed without fuss and handed the rod to Nathi. The parrot was not wholly stupid and hopped up onto her shoulder, well out of the way as Nisa crouched down beside the chair. Both of them cringed when he went to cast backwards, but this time, it didn't catch!

Nathi whipped the line forwards. It snaked through the air with a satisfying hiss, until the hook caught on one of his back wheels. The sudden jolt almost tipped him into the river!

"He's only gone and caught himself!" one of the fishermen spluttered and creased up, but the mood had shifted and none of the others laughed at his wise crack.

"You'd better hope he gives up soon, or he'll have you both in the river! I hear her sort don't swim too good neither, coming from the desert. So you be careful Miss. There's hippos in there!" he yelled, not knowing when to quit. This time the rest of them stared at him in stone cold silence. Even he stopped laughing as Nisa primly marched up to the end of the jetty.

"Oh dear," Nathi gulped, "Now you've gone and done it, mate."

Without looking back, little Nisa dived right into the river, there and then, in front of them all. Nathi cheered as she bobbed back up to the surface, to a round of applause from the fishermen.

"Hippos don't scare me one bit, if you remember. Which I'm sure some of *your sort* do!" she shouted and swam back towards the bank like an otter.

They did remember too. Or at least they'd heard about it, if they hadn't seen it with their own eyes. How she once tamed a hippo and brought it right into the village, pulling a cart!

The fisherman who leant them the rod hurried over to help Nisa back onto dry land.

"Well done, Miss. You showed him, alright!" he declared loudly and turning to Nathi added, "And as for you, we'll make a fine fisherman out of you yet. I'm sorry. It weren't your fault, you know? That rod is broke, is all."

"Thank you for saying so. It's very kind of you," mumbled Nathi, hanging his head.

"No it isn't and it weren't very kind of me to lend you a duff rod neither. Tell you what! To make it up to you, why don't you come by my cottage tomorrow and I'll have a nice, new rod made just for you. How about that?" he asked.

"That'd be brilliant! Thanks mister," Nathi brightened up, "But which is your cottage?"

"Blue door, three windows. Nearest one to the river," he pointed it out in the distance.

A wet Nisa helped to push the chair back to the village, whilst Nathi spun the wheels.

"Nisa? You did know that the hippos would all be resting up at the lake, now that the rains have started, didn't you?" Nathi checked.

"Well yes, to be honest," she admitted.

"But did it occur to you, that the river's still full of crocodiles?" he asked.

"Oh cripes! I hadn't thought of that," she stopped pushing briefly, to shudder instead.

"Oh Nisa. Will you ever learn, to think before you act?"

"I think I just did," she thought for a second, "And my dad would've killed me!" she gasped.

"Not if the crocodiles had got to you first," Nathi began to chuckle and they laughed all the way home after that, but Nisa felt that she really had learned her lesson, at last.

Nisa rushed through any chores she'd been given that day. There wasn't that much to do, since her parents were running out of ideas to punish her with, finally. She was finishing mucking out the donkeys when Jasmine appeared, blocking out the light as she stood in front of the doors.

Donkey calmly walked forwards for his usual fuss from her, while Jenny, his girlfriend hung back. She was still unsure of this monstrous great creature, whether he trusted it or not.

"I was beginning to wonder what happened to you, since I

haven't seen you for a while," the dragleon began, "But I saw your father just now and he explained why you've been so busy."

"I bet he did and yes, before you ask, I have learned my lesson. How are you?" asked Nisa.

"Sorry, but I must get this done because I'm going to the lake with Nathi once I've finished. He'll be waiting for me. He wants to try his hand at fishing again," she went on to explain, secretly dreading it, "We thought we'd practice out at the lake, which should be quieter than the river."

"Oh, fishing is it? That could be fun. I've never been to that little lake either. Am I invited?"

Nisa quickly rinsed her arms in a bucket of water and reached up to hug Jasmine.

"Of course you are. Nathi will be chuffed to bits, but please don't laugh at him when he tries fishing. I'm afraid he finds it a bit," Nisa searched for the right word, "Difficult. He'll keep trying though. You know what he's like, when he gets an idea into his head."

"I do. It's one of the things I like about him. Such a nice boy. I've been back at that patch of scrub between the two streams, where we went the other day. There's been a bit of damage done to some of the trees and the new growth, by elephants of all things. No traces of leopard this time though. Perhaps it followed us back here, having seen us out in the woods?"

"It saw me alright, right outside my own bedroom. Never mind out in the woods."

The dragleon walked very carefully to the outskirts of the village, with a rather cheeky Nathi and Nisa teasing her about flimsy shop porches and knocking down walls and such.

"I doubt even I could knock those down," Jasmine joked, admiring the stout new gateposts.

They skirted around the ring of thorns and entered the village again by the river road, through another set of massive gateposts. They soon found the fisherman's cottage and Nathi trundled up to knock on the blue door.

"Oh hello there. Glad you called by, and I see you've got company too. Hello again Miss," he greeted Nisa, "And um, Jasmine! Last time I saw you was dancing through the streets. Or what was left of 'em, by the time you'd finished," he chuckled, winking at Nathi and Nisa. The children giggled behind their hands, while Jasmine raised her eyes. Would she ever live it down?

"That was some conga though and a right good night. What a dance! What a party! Hope it happens every year, I do and all thanks to you, I say. Now then, hang on a minute, mate," he said to Nathi, retreating back indoors, "Be with you in a tick."

He returned with a brand spanking new rod and a whole reel of line.

He'd even pierced a leather strip with some hooks for Nathi to practice with, more safely.

"Oh that's so kind of you. Thanks. It's great! How can I ever repay you?" Nathi babbled.

"You just bring me the first big fish you catch with it. Mind, no tiddlers and if I was you, I'd try bending my elbow when I cast back, then straightening my arm, quick like, when I cast out," the fisherman hinted, tapping the side of his nose. Having seen his efforts of the day before, he figured the boy needed all the help he could get. He wasn't far wrong either, as it turned out.

They walked and wheeled back to the track that led directly to the lake. Jasmine kept staring into and sniffing at the forest, where it crept up to one side of the path. She didn't see or smell anything though. No toffee popcorn, which is what leopards smell like, strangely, but they do.

The little lake looked beautiful at this time of year. Jasmine clasped her hands together and sighed at the sight of it. Purple irises speared up from the damp earth all around her.

The reeds by the shore had burst open at their tips with fluffy white heads of seeds. The water lilies were in full bloom, pink and cream, with sparkling darts of red and blue damselflies flitting in amongst, to settle on their fleshy, floating leaves. Tangles of yellow Kingcups flowered along the steeper banks, sheltering sleepy frogs. The pod of hippos lolling in the lake caused gentle waves to slosh up through the reed beds, putting kingfishers and flocks of small finches to flight. While the lake's pair of fish eagles threw back their heads and called to one another from the only two trees, which stood apart on the far shore.

Nathi kept on trying to cast the line back and Nisa kept freeing the hook from the ground or from plants, for him to try again.

"I am bending my elbow like he said, but in my chair I'm not tall enough to do it properly. Here. You try," he said, passing the new rod to Nisa in disgust.

She wasn't sure what to do for the best. While she secretly wanted to have a go, she didn't want to make Nathi look bad, if she proved to be any good at it.

"I'm no higher standing up than you are sitting in your chair though," she settled for, "Why don't you sit on Jasmine's shoulders and try? You'll be higher up than the fishermen then even."

"If that's alright with you?" Nathi at least, thought to check with Jasmine.

"Of course. Come on up, by all means," Jasmine agreed, hoisting him onto her shoulders, "I'll hold onto your legs, shall I?" she suggested and . . . . .SWISH!

The line snaked backwards, until he whipped back around and sent it hissing out over the lake. The hook landed with a delicate "plop!" and a cheer from Jasmine and Nisa.

"I did it! I did it!" Nathi squealed, jigging up and down on the dragleon's shoulders.

"Now reel it back in slowly, like the fishermen do," Nisa encouraged him, willing it to work.

He got so far and no further, as the hook caught on something in the lake. He tried reeling in harder and watched in dismay as some of the lilies lifted clear of the water.

"Oh no. Now what am I going to do?" he grumbled, "You couldn't…?"

"Clear it? Of course," Jasmine offered, lowering him into his chair, "I like the look of those water lilies anyway. I was wondering what they taste like."

She began wading out towards the snagged lilies. A sudden swell lapped at their feet, as the "Harrumphing" hippos rushed and sploshed to get out of her way.

"Ooh hoo hoo hoo. There's definitely fish in here," giggled Jasmine, as barbels began to nibble at her scales under the water, "Eeh hee hee hee, it tickles. Ooh hoo hoo! It's quite nice actually," she decided, dragging the water lilies back with her talons and slopping them onto the shore.

"Thanks Jasmine. What would we do without you?"

"You can find and free the hook without me for a start, while I enjoy a little snack here."

After a great deal of fiddling and faffing about, the children managed to free the hook and untangle the line from the tangle of plant stems. By the time they'd finished, the dragleon had polished off the flowers and begun to nibble on the fleshy leaves too.

"You don't normally eat leaves, do you?" asked Nisa.

"No, but these are really rather good and the flowers are

nearly as nice as your mum's doughnuts!" Jasmine declared, standing up to lift Nathi onto her shoulders again, "Now mind the hippos, won't you? We don't want you catching one of those. I wonder what the fisherman would say, if we turned up with one of them on his doorstep," she mumbled with her mouth full.

"Cripes! Now that is a whopper!" Nisa risked a chuckle, "And mind the water lilies too."

"Ooh, no. You can catch as many of these as you like," Jasmine managed, between mouthfuls.

Nathi cast the line out perfectly this time and slowly withdrew the hook, without snagging anything. He did it again and again, beaming at his own success.

"Why not try from your chair again. See if it works better, now you've got the hang of it."

His parrot leaned over to rub the top of its head on Nathi's cheek, as if congratulating him.

The dragleon lounged on her back by the shore, crossing her legs at the knee and draping a taloned hand in the shallow water.

"Nisa, can you get the hook for me please? Sorry."

"Of course. No need to be sorry. Why are those water lilies moving, Jasmine? Are you actually calling them over somehow, so you can eat them?" Nisa tried not to laugh, handing Nathi the hook, "Show me your talons. You're doing it somehow. I know you are."

Jasmine smiled like a crocodile and lifted her empty hand, but Nisa had guessed right. She had been trying to summon the water lilies, using only the magic of her mind to lure them within reach. And it worked! The spreading plants were indeed edging towards her, only to be eaten.

"It saves me having to wade in and reach around in the muddy water, upsetting the hippos all over again. Poor things," the dragleon protested. She felt rather pleased with her new trick; of moving any plants it seemed, without even having to touch them. It clearly had a number of uses.

"OH! Sorry Nisa. You couldn't free the hook again, could you?"

"Since when have you cared how the hippos are feeling?" argued Nisa, "Here it is."

"It's my trick and up to me how I choose to use it. Like so!" Jasmine smiled triumphantly, raising a slopping mass of plant life out of the lake. She began to eat it by picking off the flowers.

"OHUH!" Nathi shouted, frustrated, "Nisa?"

"It's okay, I'll get it," she replied, still watching Jasmine, who had finished all the flowers and started eating the leaves again, which was odd, "I wonder why they float on the surface of the water like that. Wouldn't leaves normally sink, after a while?"

"Thanks. Yes they would. Right! This time," Nathi sneered.

"They keep sort of popping inside my mouth," Jasmine tried to think how best to put it. "It feels funny, like lots of little bursting bubbles, but really nice, so you don't want to stop."

"OH! It's no use! I just can't do it any more!" yelled Nathi, throwing down the rod.

Nisa got up, found the hook and rolled up the line on her way back to him.

"I can only do it from Jasmine's shoulders and she won't be around all the time, will she?" Nathi blustered, in something of a temper by now.

"You're better at tying the hook. We'll just have to think of a way around it. You usually do. Something will come to you, sooner or later. You'll see," Nisa tried to reassure him.

"I think that's quite enough of that for one day now anyway.

Don't you?" the dragleon decided, throwing the stalks and stems back into the lake, where they started growing again, immediately. She burped out loud and none too daintily either.

"Jasmine!" gasped Nathi, thinking it was funny. At least it brought a smile back to his face.

They joined her in lounging on the shore of the pretty little lake, lazily watching this or that, whenever something moved, took flight, or rippled the water's surface.

"Mum reckons we've got mice behind the new kitchen units," Nathi mentioned idly.

"Ha! She thinks she's got problems? I've got elephants in my new acacias!" Jasmine scoffed, "She's welcome to swap her mice for my elephants, any time!" which made them chuckle.

"Would your elephants fit behind her kitchen units though?" Nisa wondered, giggling.

"Hmmm. It would make one heck of a mess, I suppose," Jasmine thought about it.

One of the fish eagles launched from its tree on spreading wings. After a couple of powerful strokes, it sailed out over the lake, gliding effortlessly. It swooped low and swung its talons forward, plucking a struggling perch from just below the surface. The eagle had to beat its wings heavily to lift the slippery fish clear of all the cascading water. The big perch fought and flapped against the sudden rush of fresh air on its face, for the first and last time. And just like that, it was gone from the lake, for ever more.

"Wow! That looked so easy, out there on the water. Boomph! Just like that," Nathi gasped.

At precisely that moment, and there is no delicate way of putting this, the dragleon farted! It was long and loud and surprised even Jasmine, clearly shocked by her own body's bad behaviour.

The children stared at each other in disbelief, before screaming with laughter.

"Ooh, I'm ever so sorry. I don't know what came over me! Really I don't," Jasmine apologised, blushing bright pink, all over.

Once they'd finally recovered from their fit of giggles, Nathi began to think out loud.

"If I was out on the water, it shouldn't matter that I'm not high up. When I cast back, the hook would land on the surface of the water and float like the leaves do, so I could cast forwards easily."

"Can anyone else smell water lilies because . . ." Nisa managed before Jasmine interrupted, with another explosive fart!

It was even louder and if anything, longer than the one before. Her face scrunched up with the sheer effort of finishing it. Both children fell about laughing, rolling around and giggling. Eventually they recovered, although Jasmine hadn't helped with yet more heartfelt apologies.

"It must be the leaves, but I can't think why. They were so nice to eat," she excused herself.

"Of course! The bubbles you liked, that pop in your mouth? You're *farting*," Nisa whispered that word, "Because you've swallowed so much air, trapped within the leaves. That's what makes them sit on the surface, floating like they do. It must be."

"That's it! They sit on the surface, where I need to be to fish, maybe as well as anyone else too. Nisa, I need a boat! That should do it. Why not?" Nathi erupted with his bright idea.

"Brilliant! I knew you'd think of something. Now we've just got to get you a boat, from somewhere. And I really can smell water lilies, you know?" added Nisa, sniffing the air.

"Errr! That's disgusting. The smell's coming from Jasmine's flowery farts!" Nathi burst out, less concerned with manners than Nisa had been.

He tried to cover his nose while roaring with laughter, which was never going to work, when the dragleon really let rip, with yet another thunderous fart!

A flock of drinking doves took flight, which had the children howling all over again. Nathi later swore the ground shook, while Nisa said it sent ripples right out across the lake.

"Here Jasmine," she screeched, "If you tried to take off now, you'd fly like a bird, for sure!"

"Yeah you could be half way home, on just one of those farts!" Nathi added.

Jasmine rather doubted it, but decided to give it a go, just for fun. She stuck out her tail, waggled her bottom and spread out her stubby, rose petal wings, waiting for another one.

"Let's see, shall we? Ooh. Here we go. Yes, wait for it!" she chuckled, "Clear at the rear!"

She actually took off about three feet from the ground, with a great big silly grin on her face.

All three of them rolled around in fits of laughter, until their sides ached and the ground was smothered with freshly grown irises and tangles of kingcups, most of which they flattened!

The journey home took longer than they thought. Jasmine kept holding them up, unexpectedly. Or rather, the children kept stopping to fall about laughing.

"At least there's no need to worry about getting home late, because they'll know we're on our way, for sure. They'll be able to hear us coming from miles away!" Nisa joked.

"They'll be able to smell us coming, if the wind's in the right direction," Nathi laughed so hard, he fell out of his chair at that one. He was still laughing as he struggled back into it, which didn't make it any easier.

They were being watched. From his perch up in the trees, the leopard tried to make sense of their strange behaviour. It paid to understand your menu options, he'd found. That one for instance, looked injured and easier to catch, yet still quite plump.

The dragleon caught the faintest whiff of toffee popcorn, which could only mean one thing.

She decided not to take any chances, now that the light was fading. Grabbing hold of the handles on the back of Nathi's chair, she rushed back towards the village, juddering him to bits. It was all Nisa could do to keep up, while Nathi loved his rough ride. It was almost sunset by the time she got them safely home. There was a supper of bread and stew already waiting for Nisa, but all too soon it was time for bed. She did her best to put it off, distracting her parents by prattling on about the day's events. It didn't work for long though. Her mother insisted she go to bed. Now!

"Ooh, Daddy, hasn't the mantis got really fat, since she ate that other one? She's huge now."

"I said NOW, Nisa!"

She lit the candle and got down on her hands and knees to look across the floor.

Reaching up and around the corner carefully, Nisa took the lid off her laundry basket.

She didn't know if house snakes ever ate scorpions, but you never knew your luck.

She ran for it, terrified of her toes being snipped and stabbed by the scorpion. She leapt up onto her bed and pulled the covers up around her, wondering where they might find a boat for Nathi, while she sailed on her way, slowly but surely, off to the land of nod.

Waking up to the sound of steady rain, she found it hard

to move her hand. It took some effort, it really did. Only then did she realise that the house snake had slid into her bed in the night and snuggled up next to her, for warmth. She stroked his long, black body. He shifted his weight a little and slithered up to tickle her chin with his flickering, forked tongue.

"Aah see? I told Mummy you'd be friendly," she yawned, stroking him some more.

It rained for three whole days and more after that, which dampened everyone's spirits.

Her father fetched some corn, a whole lot of corn, for Nisa and her mother to grind endlessly, while he set to crushing sugar cane, out in one of their storage sheds.

School was cancelled and for once, Nisa wished it hadn't been, fed up with grinding corn.

Rain dripped and dribbled off thatched and tin roofs all around the village, to gather in puddles on lanes made of hard-packed earth. Before long, the muddy puddles spread and broke their banks, to trickle through the streets as grubby, slow moving streams. By the time the miserable rain had finally stopped, the whole village was awash with mud.

Nisa went to call on Nathi, who would be housebound until the streets began to dry out.

She joked that he could practice fishing from his own front door now, but he didn't seem to get it, or find it very funny. Not even when she paddled up and down on the spot, sploshing about in the mud in her bare feet. She carried on talking to him anyway, over the doorstep, telling him how their mantis had laid two weirdly pretty egg cases, out of froth that came from her bottom. They'd hardened now, but were still very delicate, her dad said. So she wasn't allowed to bring one over to show him, or she would have.

"When all this has cleared up some, I could come and have

a look," he mumbled.

"I had an idea of where we might borrow a boat," Nisa tried, hoping it would cheer him up.

"I couldn't think of anything and then it rained."

"Dad said there'd be no harm in asking. So I'm on my way now, to ask the old boatman. He tows a canoe behind his ferry in case of emergencies, whatever they are. He used to let my dad cross the river in it, for nothing," she babbled, having already thought it all through. There wasn't much else to do whilst grinding boring corn, except think about stuff.

"Oh, nice one! Only, shouldn't it be me who asks, since it is for me?"

"No it isn't, because I want to do this for you. Dad says the boatman was nice to him before anyone else was, so he's always giving him stuff, now that he can. They're good friends, so the boatman might be happier helping me. Besides, who else could lend us a boat?"

She had a point, Nathi had to admit and said he'd keep his fingers crossed, watching the sunshine return from his front door, while Nisa headed off to the river jetty.

The old boatman wasn't there. So she sat down and waited for him, watching the fishermen fail to catch anything, unlike a black and white kingfisher.

It hovered out over the swollen river, dropping down into the water with scarcely a plop, every so often. He caught plenty of tiddlers, one after the other. As the kingfisher plopped down into the river again, Nisa noticed a swirl on the surface, speeding up towards the spot. The little bird burst up from the water, which exploded with spray behind it.

"Oh no!" she squeaked in horror.

The crocodile's hard snout hit the kingfisher, sending it spinning across the river. It landed flat on outstretched wings, flapping wetly across the surface.

The waters behind it bulged in a speeding wave as the crocodile surged towards it, still frantically flapping away. Nisa stood up, willing it on.

"Go on! Take off! Fly! Just fly!" she begged, but it seemed the bird just couldn't.

She could hardly watch as the crocodile gained on the kingfisher, closer and closer, until the sweeping wave lifted the bird up ahead of it, just enough, for the poor little thing to take off.

It whirred away to safety at the very last minute and with scarcely a ripple, a knobbly, flat log broke the surface behind it and blinked, left to wonder where it had gone.

Nisa felt like punching the air and cheering, but the boat appeared at last.

So she waved like mad to the boatman instead as he pulled over, happy to see her as ever.

Some time later, she came splashing back through the streets.

Thabo slid around the side of a hut, wondering why she looked so pleased with herself.

"He said yes! We can borrow his canoe! So long as we stay out of the river! He'll even tug it up to the lake for us, where we'll be safer," she yelled ahead, running back up the lane.

"That's great! Did he say when?" Nathi yelled back from his front door. Not that he'd been eagerly awaiting her return of course. Not that he'd admit to, anyway.

Thabo listened in with his back pressed flat against the hut, eavesdropping.

Nisa pulled up, almost out of breath, having run back all the way from the river.

"Anytime," she huffed and puffed with her hands on her muddy knees, "He said he'll leave the, canoe tied up. "Moored" is what he actually said, but I didn't know what that meant, so he said it meant tied up, where the lake drains into the river. A few fish, is all he wanted, for doing it."

"That's great! But I'm going to have to catch a lot of fish, to pay people back for all this."

"Let's hope so," Nisa replied, standing up straight and managing a smile.

Thabo was smiling too, as he usually did at the prospect of making mischief.

"What could a cripple want with a boat anyway? Or a bush girl?" he sneered, who belonged in the desert where there was no water, so they never learnt to swim, his dad said! Thabo thought about it, deciding to bide his time and steal their stupid boat, as soon as he got half a chance.

"Don't suppose Nathi can swim either, come to think of it. So maybe I'll just put a hole in it, so it sinks. While I watch," he grinned wickedly.

Chapter Six

Jasmine woke up with a nagging feeling that she'd heard elephants in the distance, during the night. Perhaps her violets had been telling her tales while she slept. They did that sort of thing, but she hoped it was just a dream, because it could be a nightmare if they'd been in her new patch of forest again. Elephants could do a lot of damage to the trees, when they put their minds to it.

She wasn't sure what she could do about them either, given that the cows were about as big as her and the bulls were even bigger. There'd be quite a few of them too, so she'd be outnumbered.

She rolled over onto her back in her glade of African violets, yawning to greet the new day.

"I guess repairing any damage already done would be a good place to start. So I'd better get over there and get on with it, hadn't I?" she said to a chameleon in the branches above. It swivelled its mad eyes around and swaying back and forth, stepped back into hiding amongst the leaves.

"Fat lot of help you are, but that's hardly your fault," she stretched and got up, "And thank you all for keeping watch over me," she said to the violets on the ground around her, well aware that they couldn't understand a word she was saying, any more than chameleons could.

Jasmine set off for a breakfast of delicious pollen and lots of it. After eating her fill and staining her nose quite yellow, she began to walk through her woods, hoping against hope that the elephants had left them well alone.

Bush babies bounced back to their holes in the trees as she passed by. They'd been to the baobabs in the night, sipping nectar from their trumpet flowers and catching the moths they attracted. She couldn't help smiling as she looked up at their bat ears and cute, gremlin faces, gawping back down at her with black, saucer eyes from the tangled branches above. Flowers popped up around her, to show how pleased she was to see them.

"Ooh. They're new," Jasmine was delighted to see springhares, hopping back to their new burrow, "And you're very welcome around here too," she said to their bouncing backs.

The springhares stopped and turned their blocky heads to look at her, as if they knew she was talking to them, but couldn't quite understand her. They thought better of it and scurried underground, safe inside their burrows for the rest of the day.

Impala raised their heads and kudu craned their necks to watch her walking by. At least they no longer bolted at the mere sight of her.

"Perhaps they're getting used to me at last, around here, anyway," she sighed with a warm glow of contentment, which caused the nearest trees to blossom, quite beautifully.

The birds of the forest had begun to stir, except for an owl, returning bleary-eyed to its roost.

Soon the woods were filled with birdsong, which sounded lovely to anyone who didn't speak songbird. Anyone who did could tell they were hurling abuse and threats at each other in the foulest language they could possibly think of, however sweet it sounded to the untrained ear.

A sudden flash of movement caught her eye, as something tiny dashed past her feet.

Looking down she noticed a network of neat paths, criss-crossing the forest floor. Each had been cleared of any twigs, grass or leaves, to form a perfect little runway.

The dragleon couldn't resist placing some dry grass across one of the paths. She sat back on her coiled up tail to watch and wait.

A blur of movement sped towards the spot, haring along the trail like a clockwork toy. It stopped short, showing itself to be an elephant shrew, rounder than a rat, with a triangle head and long legs like a tiny antelope. It stared at the blocked path with glistening black eyes that looked too big for its head, scenting the air with its long, wibbly-wobbly nose.

Having reached a decision, the elephant shrew began bustling the offending grass out of her way, pushing and pulling until her precious path was tidy once more. She scampered back and forth a few times like a little busy-body, making sure her way was clear. Finally satisfied, she sped off about her business at breakneck speed, which was how they seemed to do everything.

The dragleon sighed and clasped her hands together. Pale yellow flower spikes speared up from clumps of slender leaves, which had been growing steadily either side of her.

She rose onto all fours and marched off through her marvellous, magical woodland home, happily humming away to herself. Everything looked green and seemed to be growing well. Nothing needed her attention, not even touching up. It all seemed just about perfect, until she reached the new patch of scrubland, that she'd been giving the dragleon treatment.

"Oh dear," she said aloud, looking across the stream. It had also been given the elephant treatment, by the look of things, because it looked like a battlefield now, with the elephants declaring war on the trees, and winning.

Most of her green grasses, newly planted vines and tender new shoots had gone. Dents in the dust were all that remained to show where they'd once been, like so many shallow graves.

Saplings had been bulldozed by bulging elephant foreheads,

bending until they broke, snapped at their bases or wrenched from the ground altogether. Their pale, twisted roots looked starved and suffering, like old bones picked clean by vultures and crows.

Whole branches of acacia trees had been snapped off and stripped of their leaves. They lay like the fallen, strewn about the floor in the dust and left for dead. Some still clung to their mother trees, frayed and splintered at the join, bent down at awkward angles.

The trunks of tall fever trees had been gouged by probing tusks; their yellow bark tugged up and stripped off in long, ragged tatters. Only their topmost branches survived, still fluttering with delicate, lime green leaves.

There were elephant footprints everywhere, some large, some smaller and some where they'd dug their toenails into the dirt, so they could do more damage still. Cannonball droppings littered the ground, ranging in size from big enough to even bigger, some of them kicked to smithereens across the sand. A herd of mixed ages then, from old maids she must be wary of, to youngsters that would scream and stamp and flap their ears, but follow their mother's lead, in the end. There didn't seem to be any massive bulls tagging along with the herd, which was something at least.

The dragleon stayed strangely calm. This was not the time to be losing her temper. She was on a healing mission and her adopted trees would not be healed by angry, vengeful thoughts.

The time for that would come later, if the elephants came back.

Jasmine stepped from tree to tree, feeling the damaged trunks and half-snapped branches for any sign of life. In some the sap still rose, weakly. Others would dry out and die in the sun, bleached bare like standing skeletons.

68

Only the mopane trees, with bitter bark and leaves, had escaped the elephant onslaught.

"What if they decide to cross the stream? It cannot be allowed to happen. My whole forest home reduced to this," she fretted, "I don't think so!"

"Happy thoughts," she forced herself to smile and set out to repair what trees she could.

Wherever the slightest sign of life or stirring sap remained, the dragleon laid her talons on the trunk, or clasped the stricken branch, willing them to survive with all her might.

She moved from one stricken tree to another. It felt as if the blood coursing through her veins could somehow hear the sap and speak to it, creeping and seeping up through the trees.

It was hot and thirsty work. She kept trundling back and forth to the stream for a drink. Slowly but surely throughout the day, the dragleon worked her magic, working her way through the damaged scrub and repairing whatever she could. Clumps of grass began to sprout, here and there, wherever she had success, until she came to the marula tree, her favourite since sharing its fruit with the children. Broken! At that point Jasmine forgot about healing and finally lost her temper.

Seething, she settled down to wait instead, before the light began to fade. She hid in the bushes on the far side of the stream, all but invisible, blending in with the plants all around her. Jasmine practiced her powers, using her mind to move branches, even from a distance. She got better at it too. Soon she could bend two branches at a time, then three and even four. Or she could sway the mopane saplings and rattle whole bushes, when she wanted to. There were a few places that looked promising, for what she had in mind. Places where the trees grew closer together or their branches grew closer to the ground. She practiced on them in particular, until she'd practiced quite enough.

The dragleon waited some more. Dusk came and went as baboons settled down, barking in some distant trees. Twilight faded fast as a pair of porcupines shuffled off into the scrub. The forest bathed in the silvered light of the moon, by the time the chittering bats came out to play. Still the dragleon lay in wait, listening. The stars came out, blinking between the clouds. An owl set out on silent wings, when suddenly she heard them. A youngster squeaked in the herd and got told off by an older sister, which was warned by the calf's mother, in turn. Elephants!

After that she heard nothing. Not a peep. How could anything so big move so quietly? Jasmine could see perfectly well in the dark, but even so, she didn't make out their grey bulk in the grey gloom, not until they were nearer than she knew how.

The elephants had gathered around a stand of battered acacia trees, milling around with flapping ears and raised trunks, trying to decide what to start on.

Jasmine had practiced on those same trees earlier. It was high time they got their own back.

She leaned forwards with slanted eyes and held out her talons, reaching out to the trees.

Their lowest branches began pulling back, slowly creaking and curling around. The dragleon forced them further back still; as far back as she dared, until she feared they'd snap!

One of the elephants let out a squeak. Trees didn't move on their own like that and yet…?

Suddenly, Jasmine let go.

The branches whipped back, slapping several elephants at once.

They screamed and turned on their nearest neighbours, thinking it was them.

The dragleon raised some higher branches, as high up as she dared.

As the elephants squabbled amongst themselves, she let them go as well.

They swished back down, lashing them across their grey backs.

One cow pushed into another, trumpeting loudly. A third got bumped from behind and squealed, prodding the elephant in front with her tusks. It turned around, roared and pushed right back at her. Branches rained down on the herd, swatting them with showers of twigs, while others swiped back and forth, slapping their faces and smacking their legs. More and more branches joined in the fray as Jasmine, crazed, conducted the trees like an orchestra, bent on revenge.

The adults trumpeted madly. Youngsters screamed in surprise. The calves began to squeal with fear, but Jasmine couldn't help that. She kept going, kept working, kept fighting.

The herd panicked, screaming and trumpeting, whirling around, whipped and swatted by a foe they couldn't fight, could barely see in the dark and couldn't begin to fathom.

A calf got knocked to the ground by its mother, as she spun to face whatever slapped her. The calf squeaked in shock and its mother screamed, enraged. She called again, out of concern, torn between fighting nothing there and protecting her fallen baby.

Still the branches swished and walloped them, battering and beating their tough hides. The elephants bawled as they surged and shifted, stomped the calves and shouldered each other, barging around in crazed circles.

One of the calves finally broke ranks, shuffling off across the scrub, squealing as it trundled away. It was closely followed by its trumpeting mother, scared of losing her baby in the dark.

Jasmine reached out to some mopane saplings; chin raised,

straining and curling her talons.

As the calf squeaked past, they whipped it on the backside, making it trumpet for the first time in its little life. Its mother went berserk, charging into the springy saplings after her frightened calf, suddenly horsewhipped and screeching in shock and fear and rage, all rolled into one.

Others in the herd turned tail and ran; anything to get out of this hellish place that made no sense at all. As they barrelled almost blindly through the darkness, screeching and squalling, Jasmine made the shrubs and saplings whack them on their way.

She'd broken the herd. Trumpeting elephants ran off in different directions and still she tripped and swiped at the stragglers, bending the trees and shrubs to her will. Jasmine finally began to calm down, as the last of the herd screamed off into the distance.

Confused and bruised they may be, which was unfortunate, but the elephants would not be back.

Exhausted by so much effort, the dragleon slumped down on the spot to sleep it off. She slept and slept and slept some more, curled up with her talons twitching, while she dreamed.

She woke up to something blobby, patting her on the cheek. She opened her eyes and could only smile, at the weird little face looking back down at her. A chameleon was catching flies that dared to land on her face, the sticky blob on the end of its tongue plopping onto her scales.

"Why thank you," she said, rising with a stretch and realising it was light already, "I must've slept right through," she yawned, with a nagging feeling that something wasn't quite right.

It was dawn, as it should be, so Jasmine waddled over to see what damage had been done last night. Not much at all as it turned out, but she noticed how well her grasses had grown back, all over the place it seemed. That couldn't be right. They couldn't have grown back so thickly, so quickly. The branches she'd set to repair only yesterday, were already knitting together. Some had even sprouted leaf buds, about which she was pleased, if confused. Surely it was too soon.

"Oh dear. I must've been tired. I've slept even longer than I thought. Ooh, that's weird. I've missed a whole day and another night too! I must have," it dawned on her.

Chapter Seven

After a couple of sunny days, the mud began to dry and crack. So long as he steered clear of any stubborn puddles that remained, Nathi could venture out once more.

Nisa went to speak with the boatman. The river road went nowhere near the forest, so she was allowed. It led through perfumed jasmine bushes, which appeared when she'd first named the dragleon. She passed by both the acacia trees, there to remind her of unhappy times. One had grown from a dragleon talon, bitten off by that big old mean hyena, while the other had sprouted when she'd roared at the villagers, before they'd all become friends. Nisa didn't like those two trees, but the birds and some small, stripy squirrels did, so Jasmine let them be.

She padded along the jetty to greet the old boatman, asking if he'd remembered the canoe.

"Yes of course. Seeing as it's for you. Left it moored up by the lake, only yesterday," he answered cheerfully, "Mind, you only go with a grown-up. You promise me?"

"Thank you and I promise. Seeing as it's for you," Nisa added, almost cheekily.

"Now, don't you be mocking me. A second goat and another dog's gone, I heard. It was two chickens, only last night! So you be careful. The sooner them gates is up the better, if you ask me."

"Chickens too now! It's getting bolder, but does Jasmine count as a grown-up?" asked Nisa.

"Why yes, of course. I should think she counts as three of four, if you know what I mean."

She didn't exactly, but wasn't about to let that stop her,

not once she'd got permission, of sorts. So Jasmine, Nisa and Alice from school went to watch Nathi try fishing from a boat. It was quite exciting, since nobody from their village had ever tried fishing from a boat before.

"I think you're very brave," Alice gushed, which earned her a swift glare from Nisa.

Jasmine saw it and smiled to herself, but mostly she was sniffing at the forest along the edge of the lake road, to see if she could pick up any trace of leopard. Thankfully she didn't and they soon reached the lake, without mishap.

Nisa untied the canoe and Jasmine towed it by its rope, while they walked around the shore.

"I reckon this should do. About here," Nathi decided, reaching a spot without reeds.

He politely refused Alice's help and lowered himself to the ground. When she went to hold the back of his chair, his parrot nipped her finger. She sucked at it, frowning.

Using his arms Nathi hauled himself along the ground, dragging his legs behind him.

Alice looked away quickly, as if ashamed of something, which Nisa didn't like.

Getting into the canoe was harder than he thought, since it tipped towards him as soon as he put any weight on one side. Alice kindly went to hold the other side down and looked a little crestfallen, when Nathi declined her help a second time.

Eventually he got the measure of it and got in, seated and settled, all by himself.

"Ah. You couldn't give me a tow out onto the water, could you Jasmine?" he had to ask.

The dragleon was only too happy to help, but only because he'd asked. She'd long since learned that it wounded his pride if she stepped in too soon and she wouldn't do that to him. He had every right to his pride, as far as she was concerned.

He'd earned it.

Besides, there were lots of juicy water lilies further out and she'd keep the hippos at bay, once she got in the water. She started to giggle as the fish began to nibble at her again. It tickled.

"Try learning to steer and stop first, Nathi. Don't try to run before you can . . . Um, um, to race before you can, um, paddle, properly, is what I meant to say," poor Alice corrected herself and shot a pleading glance at Nisa, who was trying not to snigger behind her hand.

"You're funny, Alice. It's only a saying. I wouldn't have minded," Nathi assured her.

"Thanks. Sorry. I'm just not used to being around, you know? I'm trying," Alice pleaded.

"Then stop trying. Really, there's no need," Nisa stepped in with some well-meant advice, "If he was any more thick-skinned, he'd be a rhinoceros. You soon get used to being around him. Chair or no chair, he's just a WEIRDO!" she finished loudly, teasing him from a safe distance.

"Who're you calling a weirdo?" Nathi yelled, splashing water at them with a paddle.

The girls screamed and jumped backwards, laughing. Safely beyond the reach of any more splashes, they sat down on the grass together. It looked like they might just get on, after all.

"See what I mean? I find I don't hardly notice his chair or his duff legs any more, unless he asks for my help. I think that's the key," Nisa tried to explain as the parrot landed on her shoulder.

"I've learnt that lesson already," Alice admitted, flinching as the parrot lunged at her.

"He knows you mean well, or you wouldn't have wanted to come. He, well, we're both really pleased that you did," Nisa told her, "And sometimes even I have to remind myself what his mum and dad keep telling me; that a disease called polio damaged his legs, not me. So I shouldn't feel guilty around him, no matter what it seems he can't do. Neither should you, or anyone else."

"I suppose I thought I should try and be extra nice or something. When really there's no need, is there? And certainly not to you!" she glared at his parrot, which glared right back at her.

"Hey, you two! Look at him go! He's a natural!" Jasmine yelled over.

She lifted a slopping lily up from the lake, gazed at it greedily and took her eye off the boat.

Nathi had got the hang of paddling, alright. His arms were very strong for a boy of his age, from constantly wheeling his chair about. He was used to keeping his balance as well, so he could power the canoe through the water with more confidence than most.

He was racing along now, head down and going like the clappers, with no thought of slowing down or steering, or even watching where he was going, it looked like.

"Um. Jasmine!" Nisa shouted, pointing urgently.

"Nathi! Watch out! Look where you're going!" Alice screamed.

"Shutup! Shutup!" the parrot screeched at Alice, "Nathi! Nisa!"

"What?" muttered the dragleon, turning around sharply, once they'd got her attention.

He was heading straight for the far end of the lake, where all the hippos had gathered, as far away from Jasmine as possible, but none too happy about being so squashed up together.

"NATHI!" the dragleon roared, as soon as she spotted the danger. She surged after him.

The hippos heard her roar, which certainly got their attention.

"Whoa,oa,oa!" Nathi wailed, looking up as he careered towards the crowded hippos.

They didn't look happy about that either. He stopped paddling, but the canoe sped onwards. Jasmine powered through the water. She appeared to be charging them, the hippos decided. The girls stood up on the bank. Nathi froze with fear in the boat. The hippos panicked! The girls could hardly look. The dragleon raced after the canoe. As it slowed down, she almost had it. The hippos barrelled out of her way, as the canoe sliced right through the middle of the herd.

A tidal wave of hippos and sloshing water surged either side of it. The girls slumped with relief. The hippos whipped around on the shore, "harrumphing" their complaints and warning him by yawning widely, to show him their terrible teeth. Nathi breathed a sigh of relief, leaning back in the canoe as Jasmine took hold and stopped it.

"Oh, thank you," he gasped.

"See! I told you to learn stopping and steering. Not to RUN, before you could WALK!" Alice yelled at him. Both girls burst out laughing and fell over backwards.

The parrot, put out, flapped back onto the chair, which seemed more stable than Nisa.

"Oh very funny, I'm sure!" Nathi managed to sneer while shouting. He'd learned his lesson though and calmed down after that, learning how to steer the canoe and how to stop it, without Jasmine's help! He soon got the hang of it.

While the dragleon kept a watchful eye on him, the girls chatted together on the shore. Nisa filled Alice in on Nathi's attempts at fishing so far, which were hardly promising.

"Jasmine! Have you noticed there's a thorn tree growing in the middle of the lake now?" she shouted out, "It wasn't there a while ago and it looks kind of, out of place."

"Well? What do you want me to do about it? I shouldn't think it'll live long in the water anyway," the dragleon shouted, sputtering bits of water lily back into the lake.

"Are you sure you should be eating that, after what happened last time?" Nathi warned.

"You just stick to your paddling and such! Besides, it was really rather funny, I thought."

After a while she fetched his rod and line, before wading well out of the way.

"Please oh please, let him be good at it this time," Nisa pleaded, to no one in particular.

Nathi cast back and they held their breath.

His parrot ducked, but so far so good. He hadn't been hoisted aloft just yet.

Nathi turned and flicked forwards. The hook sailed out and over the water, landing with a plop! The parrot sat up again, relieved, while Nathi jiggled up and down in the boat. He turned around to beam at Nisa, who was standing on the shore with her hands clasped together.

"I did it! I did it!" he squealed with glee, while Alice and Nisa jumped up and down.

Nathi really had got the hang of it now, but the parrot still flinched every time he cast out, perfectly, time and time again, until the hook caught on the lake's new thorn tree.

"That's not your fault!" Nisa called out, "It's Jasmine's! She put that there and it shouldn't be."

"Oh, alright. Honestly!" the dragleon complained, wading over to free the hook.

It was well and truly entangled amongst the thorns. She simply couldn't free it, not by any normal method. The more she fiddled with it, the worse it seemed to get. She admitted defeat and laid her talons on the tree trunk instead, closing her eyes to concentrate. The whole tree flopped into the water, as if made of squiggly noodles. It sank without trace, in bits.

Alice could scarcely believe it, but the others had seen it before and didn't think it so strange.

The fish, however, thought it was marvellous! Suddenly there were all sorts of tasty tit-bits for them to nibble at, right in the middle of their lake. They shoaled towards the sinking debris, in something of a feeding frenzy.

Nathi was quick to take advantage, reeling the freed hook in fast. As soon as Jasmine got out of the way, he cast out among the feeding fish. In next to no time, the line pulled tight, very tight!

"I've got one! I've got one!" he squealed with delight and began to reel it in.

The others watched with baited breath, hoping against hope that he'd caught a fish, at last!

He'd caught one alright, a real whopper! It put up quite a fight. As he struggled to reel it in, the big barbel almost tipped him into the water, which took him by surprise. He soon recovered his balance though and carried on, yanking away, reeling in more line whenever he felt it go slack. His arms began to ache as the line got shorter and shorter, until he could see the fish, fighting against him as he wrestled it up to the surface. Finally, he managed to haul it up and into the canoe!

Everyone cheered, the girls jumping up and down and clapping on the shore.

"YES!" Nathi punched the air. He'd done it!

He went on to catch five more fish after that, though none of them quite as big as the first. He would've carried on too, trying to catch even more. Only Jasmine rather spoiled the party, having been on the water lilies again. A great big ring of bubbles erupted on the surface of the lake, all around her!

After that the fish just seemed to lose interest. They stopped biting anyway.

It was a pity the fishing party couldn't see underwater, to see what the fish were doing down there instead. It really was quite something. Fish eagles can see through the water's surface though and into the depths below. The lake's male had been keeping a lazy eye on things, from high up in his tree. All of a sudden, he snapped to attention and very nearly fell off his perch!

Nathi was so proud of himself on the way home and rightly so. It was his idea and it worked, despite a few snags along the way. They'd been snags he'd overcome though, which made his success seem all the sweeter. Jasmine and Nisa especially felt delighted for him, perhaps because they'd helped him along the way, when he'd asked for it, which felt like an honour right now.

"In future you might want to bring a basket along. To save you slopping smelly fish home on your knees, like that," Alice suggested, "Your mum'll go mad! I know mine would."

"Good idea. She won't be happy, having to wash my shorts again. Next time, I'll probably catch even more fish too, now that I'm getting good at it," Nathi almost boasted.

The dragleon kept farting all the way back, which shocked poor Alice at first. She soon joined in with their bouts of giggling though, each time Jasmine did it again.

Nathi insisted they go home the long way round, ignoring the quicker lake road. Why became clear as he trundled up the jetty on the river, calling to the boatman. He looked pleased as Punch, when the boy in the wheelchair proudly handed over two of the fish he'd caught, as agreed.

"Sorry, but I promised the first one I caught to the man who made me the fishing rod, or you could've had that as well. The rest are for my Mum," Nathi told him.

"Why! That's a big perch and not a bad sized barbel," he marvelled, "Well done, you!"

"Oh, and we tied up your canoe, right where you left it for us. Thank you, but can I borrow it again soon?" Nathi added, "Please?"

"Don't you worry little man, a bargain's a bargain. Nothing wrong in that," chuckled the boatman, "And I tell you what, how about we make a new bargain? Seeing as I love a nice bit of fish and I know you're a man of your word now. How about, that I leave the canoe up there? It's yours, so long as you bring me some of your catch, each time you go fishing in it, eh?"

"Wow! That'd be brilliant! Thanks mister. You're on!" Nathi burst out.

Grinning wider than ever, he reached forwards to shake the old man's gnarled hand.

After that, they went on to the fisherman's cottage. He seemed equally delighted when Nathi presented him with the first huge fish he'd ever caught.

"That's a right monster and no mistake!" he exclaimed, "But are you sure I can have it? They're very tasty, your barbels. I'm sure your ma would be chuffed to bits with it."

"A bargain's a bargain," Nathi repeated happily, "I never would've caught it anyhow, if it hadn't been for you, and Mum can have the rest."

They chatted away about where he'd caught the big fish and how he'd landed it, with the old man giving him the odd hint or handy tip, every now and then. The others listened patiently.

"Didn't I tell you we'd make a fine fisherman out of you? Seems like you've only gone and done it all by yourself already," he finished.

"Not all by myself," Nathi admitted, "I had a lot of help

from my friends, here."

Jasmine reached over and ruffled his hair, whether he liked it or not. She couldn't resist.

"Right, I'd better get these three home in good time for their tea tonight. We were a bit late last time. I thought their folks'd have my guts for garters. Besides, I must get back to patrol my woods. I've had elephants in my acacias. They made a right mess and took some getting rid of!"

"I bet they did! Noble creatures, but they can do a lot of damage to your trees," the fisherman agreed as Jasmine yawned widely, which brought on a final, booming fart!

"Ooh, I'm ever so sorry, and in company too," she gushed, blushing bright pink again.

He was too busy laughing to reply for a while. Yet when he did, it quite made Jasmine's day.

"Ha! We're all of us only human. Even you, miss Jasmine!"

Strangely, as he left his cottage the next morning, the fisherman would be scratching his head and wondering where all these flowers had come from, as if they'd just sprung up overnight.

Nathi's family ate like royalty that evening; grilled fish with all the trimmings. There'd been enough for all three of them and his father seemed especially proud of him, for once. His mother said she would've been just as proud, if only she didn't have to wash his shorts again.

Clearly, there was more to Alice than Nathi had given her credit for.

When Nisa got home, her mum gave her a kiss on the forehead, which surprised her.

"Your house snake friend did us proud this afternoon. He killed and ate a cobra! Right on our doorstep! It was amazing! People stood around to watch. One of the elders reckoned he stopped it coming into the house, for sure," she went rigid for a moment, just thinking about it.

"Where is he? I want to give him a cuddle, to say thank you."

"Oh I should think he's having his tea. His wife's a good cook, you know?" her mum teased.

"The snake, Mum! He likes cuddles and being stroked. He kisses my chin too," Nisa told her.

"I'm not sure I approve of that, but it was quite something to watch him in action. I was scared stiff, to tell you the truth. The cobra kept on biting him and he just took it, as if it was nothing."

"Oh no! Is he hurt?"

"I'm surprised he's not well and truly dead, but he seemed absolutely fine."

"But what happened, Mummy?" begged Nisa, pulling eagerly on her wrist.

"He just bit it on the back and sort of worked his way up to its head and swallowed it whole, still alive! I couldn't believe it! The cobra was nearly as big as he is. Its tail was wriggling around for ages, still sticking out of his mouth," her mum recalled with a shudder.

"But where did he go? Please Mummy?"

"He was so bloated, he could barely move after he'd swallowed it, but he seemed determined to slither back to your laundry basket. I even held it on its side, so he could get in easier."

"He seems to think it's his laundry basket now," Nisa reckoned.

"And he's welcome to it as far as I'm concerned, after saving us all from a cobra!"

Nisa ran into her room and reached into her laundry basket, to give him a gentle stroke from his head down to his tail. He didn't like it if you went the other way. She felt so proud of him and giggled when he flicked his tongue in and out on her wrist. It tickled.

She couldn't wait to tell her classmates all about it, tomorrow being a school day.

The family sat down to dinner when her father came home, after a long day's work in their storage sheds. He discussed going to various markets with her mother, roads permitting.

Nisa was telling her parents about Nathi getting the hang of fishing and Alice coming with them. She stopped short of talking about Jasmine's farts. They were eating dinner, after all.

"Cecily reckons they've got mice in the kitchen and asked if she could borrow Nisa's snake to get rid of them, after what he did today," her mother mentioned, winking at Nisa.

"Oh really? What was that, then?" her dad asked.

Her mum was just telling him about the snakes fighting, when Nisa dropped her spoon and SCREAMED! Suddenly terrified, staring at the doorway to her room.

Her parents whipped around on their stools, to see what the matter was.

The scorpion raised its pincers, flaring them out wide. Her mum leant over, cradling Nisa's head in her arms. Her dad stood up quickly, knocking his stool over. The scorpion flicked its stinger forwards, warning him. Nisa sat there, howling like a red faced baby, with snot bubbling down her top lip. Her father looked around for something to smack it with, but his wife beat him to it. She reached down to slip off a sandal and hurled it, with all her might. It slapped into the scorpion, sending it flying back into Nisa's room. By the time her dad had lit a candle and gone in after it, the scorpion had disappeared. Back to its hidey-hole, no doubt.

"I told you. I told you!" Nisa wailed as her mother hugged her, glowering at her husband.

"Look it's not my fault. I hardly put it there, did I? Besides, if you hadn't thrown your shoe at it, we might've managed to squash it, or at least seen which crack it went into," her dad argued.

"Just get rid of it! Plug up the gaps. I don't care! Look at her. Just look at her! How dare you expect her to sleep in there, with that vile *thing*!" her mother scolded him.

"Please Daddy, make it go away! And don't make me go to bed again, Daddy please. I can't. I'm so scared of it every night," Nisa blubbed.

Her father came over and sat down next to her, putting an arm round her shoulders.

"Nisa, how come you're best friends with a huge dragon, but terrified of a little scorpion?"

"She's not a dragon, she's the dragleon and she's nice and kind and funny," Nisa sniffled.

"Look. Your mind's playing tricks on you. Your fear of it has built this scorpion up into a real monster, but that's only inside your head. It isn't that dangerous in real life, not if you're careful. You saw how small it is, didn't you? Too small to be a real monster, surely?" he tried.

But it was no use. The danger seemed very real to a little girl, especially one who'd once seen someone stung by a scorpion, had seen the agony they'd been in. She'd even seen them in a coffin afterwards and that was that! She never wanted to see either again, scorpions or dead people!

Her dad searched her room high and low, but couldn't find it anywhere.

Her mum tried to console her, but Nisa wouldn't be

comforted, not until her dad had an idea.

"Okay, why don't I sleep in your room tonight and you sleep in here, with your mother?"

Nisa jumped at his suggestion. Her mother seemed fine with it too.

"Just for tonight, you understand," he said, "I was thinking we'd build the new room onto the side of our room, but I'll have a look tomorrow. Don't see why we couldn't build it onto Nisa's room instead and change things round a bit. What d'you reckon?" he asked his wife.

"Yes. Why not? What do you think of that, Nisa? Daddy's going to knock down the wall where the horrid scorpion lives, just for you. That'll get rid of it, once and for all!"

"Will it squash it, dead?" Nisa brightened up at the idea.

"Maybe it will, but I'll make sure it's gone for good. I promise," her dad hoped so anyway.

Later on, Nisa snuggled up to her mother and, slowly but surely, drifted off to sleep.

She was gently woken by the covers lifting, ever so slightly. She wasn't afraid though, far from it, knowing what it would be. She only hoped her mother wouldn't notice, certain she'd freak out, if she did. The house snake had found her in the night, despite her swapping beds. He wanted his usual snuggle up to her. That was all. Nisa was surprised at how fat he felt, all of a sudden. She wondered if he'd got into bed with her dad first, but found the wrong person there. The thought made her want to giggle. She tried very hard not to though, in case it woke her mum up.

Come morning, she woke up to find the snake had already gone, which was probably just as well. Over breakfast, she begged her parents to let her take him to school, to show everyone.

Her parents were having none of it though. Somehow

they didn't think her teacher would approve. So she walked without him through the new gates that Joseph had built. They looked heavy and high, their tops crowned by woven thorns to stop anything jumping over, like leopards.

School was just something Nisa had to do. The forest felt more like her classroom. Nathi was better at learning than she ever was, with stuff they learned in school anyway. Alice was better still, which sometimes got her into trouble, with the likes of Thabo. Nisa's artwork was better than anyone's though. She had a knack for drawing animals, very simply. Yet somehow they seemed almost alive, like they might step right off the paper at any moment.

They sat down on plank benches, each with their own desk, which was better than sitting cross-legged on the floor, like they used to. Since he was sitting down anyway, Nathi was given the tray that fitted smartly onto the arms of his chair. His father had made it for him.

Someone had scratched a rude insult with a crude drawing of him into the wood. He didn't want to complain, despite Nisa saying he should, convinced it must've been Thabo.

"I'm sorry, you two. Would you like to tell everyone what's so interesting, all of a sudden?"

Nathi shook his head, followed by Nisa, who was gagging to tell, but didn't.

Miss wanted to start the day with sums, which earned her a groan from most of the class.

Nathi used his paper to cover up the unkind scrawl and got on with his work, but as soon as the lesson was over, they couldn't wait to rush outside, as if running away from sums.

Break passed without much happening, which was unusual with Thabo in the playground, but he was busy with something secret, off to one side of the yard.

The next lesson was all about different words, which meant

almost the same thing, but not quite. Whatever they meant, it was better than doing sums, or maths, or numbers.

It soon became clear what Thabo had been up to during break, when he fired a large dung beetle from a home made catapult. It hit poor Alice on the back of her head! She got quite a shock and stood up quickly, screaming and stamping her feet. The beetle got all caught up in her hair. The more she tried to flick it out, the more entangled it became. Miss didn't seem to want to touch it, swiping at it with a book, which was never going to work and nearly smacked poor Alice!

The class was divided. Most of them fell about laughing, while some turned to glower at Thabo. Nisa stepped in to the rescue, having dealt with plenty of dung beetles before.

"They can't resist poo of any sort, so if you come and stand next to her, Thabo, I'm sure it'll hop off her and straight onto you instead," she sneered.

All but four of the class fell about laughing at that; Miss, the teacher, who couldn't because it wouldn't be right, Alice, who was still too busy squealing, Nisa, who was too busy sorting the dung beetle out and Thabo, who really hated being laughed at.

Nisa managed to turn the beetle over in Alice's hair and stroked its tummy a few times. As if by magic, its combed legs went limp, allowing her to tease it free.

She said she wanted to throw it at Thabo, but wouldn't do that to a dung beetle. Instead she held it up to show the teacher, who went pale, pulling a face and backing away from it.

"Just get it out of my sight," Miss hissed. She simply couldn't abide creepy crawlies, a fact that Thabo thoroughly enjoyed, from time to time.

"And Thabo! You are in a whole world of trouble, young man!" she shouted at him, "Starting with several detentions and me having some very stiff words with your parents!"

"Fat lot of good that'll do," Alice mumbled, "Well they don't care, do they?" she snapped.

"Alice! I'm warning you, I'm in no mood to suffer your cheek. I don't expect it from you."

"Sorry Miss, but I have just had a dung beetle in my hair. Thanks to HIM!" she shouted.

"I know, I know. So I'll let it pass this time. Just this once, mind."

Classes continued throughout the week, with not much else happening of note.

Most days after school, Nathi went out fishing. For bait he collected squiggly bits of the thorn bushes, which Jasmine had magically wilted. He broke them up and carried them to the lake in an old wicker basket, which Alice had rescued from her mum, before she threw it out.

Nisa and Alice went with him when they could and both his mum and dad had been to see him in action, about which he was chuffed. He used the basket to bring back his catch, but it leaked and sometimes it was scarcely big enough, because sometimes he caught loads. The old fisherman taught him how to hang his catch up on lines, to dry out in the sun, a bit like fishy laundry.

"As far from our house as possible! Or anyone else's for that matter," his mum insisted.

After a week of it, Joseph stood admiring his son's catch. He decided to ask Nisa's dad, who agreed with him. There was enough to warrant a market stall, maybe next to theirs?

And so it was decided, since Joseph had finished work on all three gates and the big new chicken coop they'd asked of him as well. He'd well and truly earned himself a day off and the very next morning, Nathi and his family would go to a market, along with Nisa and hers.

Once it was well and truly dark, the leopard stole out of the forest and slipped, in fits and starts, across the clearing. He paused for a moment, before flashing low across the path and prowling up to the ring of thorns. He could smell donkeys and chickens too, lots of chickens, all roosting together on the other side. They hadn't done that before, he was sure.

Creeping further around the thorns he smelled fish, where there hadn't been any before either. The gap in the fence had been blocked as well, by great, flat slabs of dead wood.

He tried to push through, but something metal clanked on the other side and the gates held fast. He could hear goats stirring restlessly at the noise, on the inside. The leopard licked his chops and backed up, bobbing up and down a few times to judge his leap. The gate was just that bit too high for him though, with all those thorns across the top. He raised a flickering lip to snarl silently. The tip of his tail lashed the tops of the long grass, causing clouds of pollen to billow up into the moonlight. The stirring goats alerted a couple of the village dogs, one of which growled, while the other yipped a warning to anyone who'd listen. Nobody did though, since everyone slept soundly in their beds, safe inside the ring of thorns. The leopard padded around to the next gap in the thorns bushes, which was also blocked with wood, barring him entry to the village.

He was not happy as he slunk off into the night. He was hungry.

A few hours later, Nisa's dad loaded Donkey's cart and took Jenny round to pick up Nathi and his parents, his boxes of fish and his wheelchair.

Nathi rarely went in a cart. It was fun for a while, watching the sun come up and the world go by, or waving to Nisa, waving back from the cart behind. The journey trundled on and on though. It seemed to take forever, but they got there in the end, finally parking the carts together.

Nisa told Nathi how it was, while the grown-ups used his chair to carry stuff over to three stalls, luckily all next to each other. Nisa's mum needed two stalls for all their stuff, while the third was for Nathi to sell his fish, he hoped.

"It's a big stall for your mum on her own, isn't it? Why doesn't your dad sell some things on one stall, while your mum sells her stuff on the other? Surely that would make more sense."

"It would, if only people made more sense. Some of them, a lot of them, wouldn't buy anything off my dad because he's a Bushman. Remember how people, even in our village, used to treat him and me. Not so long ago either, before Jasmine arrived?" Nisa explained, "Well there's no dragleon out here, so most of them still don't know any better."

Nathi went from looking confused, to looking a little bit nervous.

"Um, do you think they'll buy any fish off me, in my wheelchair?" he asked.

"They will if you tell them you caught it yourself. I reckon people will admire that because they'll think it was harder for you than anyone with legs. Legs they can use anyhow."

"Oh, but it wasn't though. Not once I got the hang of it," he sounded horrified now.

"If they're so blind they can't see through the colour of my skin, I doubt they'll see much past your wheelchair either. I bet you half of them talk to you like you're *really poorly* too," she teased him, "So if I were you, I'd just put up with it and smile sweetly, whilst you take their money."

"Okay, but I can use my legs for THIS though," he grinned, lifting one of them up in both hands and clubbing her with it.

He was expecting her to hit him back, like normal, but she didn't and he asked her why.

"People wouldn't like it if they saw, not round here. It's different to our village, Nathi. I'd get into real trouble if I hit you back here, no matter how much you deserved it," and he knew he did.

"Don't you worry though, because I'll get you back for it later. Oh yes!" she smiled wickedly.

"But what's it to them, if we're friends? It doesn't make any sense."

"I told you, people often don't. Especially not round here, away from our village. They won't even like it if they see us together at your stall. You won't sell as much. So I'll have to make myself scarce, probably," Nisa warned him, hanging her head.

He didn't know what to say, so he leaned over and kissed her quickly on the cheek, giggling.

"They certainly won't like that! Any more than I did!" she scoffed, "Right! That's twice I've got to get you back later. Just you wait," she snarled, playfully clenching a fist at him.

Joseph came back for them and they joined the others at the stalls, briefly.

Cecily had set up Nathi's stall with a gap between two tables for his chair, so he could reach whatever he needed to. She handed him a money belt with some change in it, smartened up his hair and brushed down his shirt, while Nathi frowned at her, for making such a fuss.

Crowds of people began filing into the market, as the first of Nisa's predictions came true.

"Good luck, Nathi, and Nisa, you come along with me," her dad ordered, as much as asking.

Nathi and Nisa exchanged very different glances. He looked shocked and she looked resigned.

"Told you," was all she said, shrugging her shoulders as her dad took hold of her hand and led her away. Nathi watched them go; confused again, trying to make sense of it all.

"Told you what?" Cecily noticed and asked him.

"That you'd split us up because people won't like seeing us together," he accused his mum.

"It's got nothing to do with what folks won't like. Just so long as they likes your fish. Heh heh! You just needs to concentrate on what you're doing today darling, that's all. Having Nisa around is bound to distract you, Sweetheart. You know how yous two get when you start mucking about," she explained, far too sweetly.

Nathi leaned sideways in his chair, looking up at her. For the first time in his life, he knew for an absolute fact, that his own mother had lied to him. He hoped it would be the last.

Chapter Eight

It would prove an eventful day at the market for both children, but for very different reasons.

People might not make much sense sometimes, but as the crowds began to bustle in they had enough sense to know good quality fish when they saw it, and at reasonable prices too.

Nathi running his own stall attracted a great deal of attention.

Many of the women, in particular, did talk to him like he must be very poorly, or possibly just plain simple. Nisa had been right about that too. So he smiled sweetly at the cooing women who ruffled his hair, while he took their money. One of them even leaned forward with both her flabby arms to pinch his "chubby cheeks". Like he was a baby! He charged her extra, which made Nisa's mum smile to herself.

"He's good with the customers, isn't he?" Cecily boasted, "I'm hardly helping at all."

"He's good with the money too. *Eh Nathi?*" Nisa's mum nodded to him, staring sideways to let him know that she'd clocked him at it, even if Cecily hadn't.

For all that, Nathi was good with the customers, and organised too, making sure there were enough fish on display and enough paper bags to wrap it in, whenever he had a moment. He had no trouble taking money and sorting out the right change and whenever his takings built up, he handed the bigger notes over to his mum, for safe keeping.

Nisa's mum was pleased, because his customers often wanted bread and vegetables to go with their fish supper. So she was doing very nicely too, thank you very much.

"Tell you what goes very well with nice, sweet corn on the cob," Nathi heard her say to one lady, "A lovely perch. Brings the flavour right out. Your husband will love it, I promise."

Sure enough, the lady's very next purchase was two of his best perch fish.

"Tell you what would go very well with your big, meaty barbel," Nisa's mum heard him advise his next customer, "Ooh, it's just delicious with sliced sweet potato, fried," he almost slurped.

Sure enough, her very next sale was a big bag of sweet potato. Smiling, she sidled over to Nathi and held up the palm of her hand.

"High five, neighbour!" she grinned, "We're working very well together, you and I. He's a fast learner, is your son," she added to Cecily, who looked like she'd almost explode with pride.

At this rate, they'd both be running right out of stock to sell, before the day was out.

The first thing Nisa wanted to do was to go and look at the horses. She wondered if the security guard would be the same one as before and if he'd remember her.

"Hello there, Missy!" he called out, waving to her cheerfully, "Have you come to look over the horses again? How's your mum today? Is she still selling those lovely doughnuts of hers?"

"Yes, Sir. Only not to you because there's no need. I brought you a couple anyway," she replied, running over to give him a small paper bag.

"Oh, so that's what she wanted them for," her father realised. To his surprise, the big security guard scooped her up under the armpits and whirled around on the spot with her.

"We've got some beauties in today. Look at that lovely grey mare over there. Here," he said, offering her a bag in return,

"You go on and give her a treat, why don't you?"

Nisa looked up at the fine horse, stroked the top of her nose and ran her palm along her neck.

"Great kid you got there," he said to her dad, who was wary around people he didn't know.

"I'm very proud of her," he admitted, "She has a way with her, around people."

"She does that. Here, don't know if you're interested, but there's some other Bushmen here today. Down by the stream. I gave 'em some of me nuts earlier. Too good for horses really."

Nisa's father was doubly amazed, at them being there at all and at the security guard, for being kind to them. People weren't, generally speaking. Far from it.

"She's real good with animals too. Will you look at that!" the guard gawped.

Nisa had moved on, to make a fuss of a fine chestnut stallion. She talked to him calmly while he nodded his head, as if agreeing with her. Soon she was stroking his cheek and his neck.

"You don't know the half of it," her dad smiled, knowingly.

"That fiery brute near took a chunk out of me earlier. Even his owner has trouble keeping him under control. He's a right handful and no mistake. Kicks like a mule and bites like a crocodile, but look at him now. She's got him eating right out of her little hand, she has. Amazing! Be careful there Missy," the guard warned her, "And thanks for the doughnuts. I'm touched, I am."

Nisa's father eventually managed to coax her away from the horses and skirted around the edge of the market, to avoid any nasty comments that might be aimed their way.

"Can I go and look at the stalls, Daddy? I don't care what people say."

"I do, but there's some people I want you to meet first," he replied, looking at the ground.

Nisa realised he was tracking. Here! At the market! He held her hand and parted some bushes, looking left and right. They walked beside a stream for a while and suddenly she saw them!

Sitting in a circle on the ground, wearing cloaks made of antelope skins, were half a dozen people that looked like her and her dad, clicking and clucking while they talked, it sounded like.

They turned around to stare, looking almost as shocked as she was. All of a sudden they beckoned them both over, making space for them to come and sit down. They seemed so happy to see her, like long lost relatives. They weren't, but her father knew them vaguely from long ago. Nisa could scarcely believe it. He even spoke their language, full of strange throat sounds and odd cloppy clicks. She looked at their happy, smiling faces, creased by the sun, smoothed by wind-blown sand and paler than most, in these parts. They were small and slender, like her dad. With high, wide cheekbones, pointed chins and almond-shaped eyes, much like her own.

One of them looked weathered and wrinkled, with hair the colour of cooled ash. She must be very old, Nisa decided and the skin she wore was different to the others. She didn't recognise it.

"What animal does that come from, Daddy?" she asked, being too polite to mention her age.

"It's the hide of an eland. Biggest and best of all the antelope and sacred to our kind. She is a Wise One and only Wise Ones can wear it these days, since the eland has become scarce," her father said and told the others what she'd asked, at which they smiled and nodded, looking at her.

One of them pointed to her feet and asked her dad something in their clicking, clacking tongue.

"He wants to know why the people he's seen around here wear shoes," her dad said.

"In case they tread on things that might hurt their feet, like thorns," Nisa explained.

Her father translated. The young man nodded and said something back, ending in a "cluck."

"He asked if you ever tread on thorns. It must hurt, if you don't wear shoes like the others."

"No I don't, come to think of it. I suppose I just watch where I'm walking instead."

Her father translated, clopping his tongue and coming back with a further question.

"He wants to know why the others tread on thorns. Don't they watch where they're walking?"

"They don't have to I guess, because they're wearing shoes," Nisa began to feel a bit lost.

"He asked if it costs you any money, or even thought, to watch where you're walking."

"No, I suppose not. I never really have to think about it," Nisa realised.

"He says the difference is that they have to pay money for shoes, which is silly. They could spend it on something more worthwhile, if only they watched where they put their feet."

The Bushmen fell about laughing, even her dad and a smile spread across Nisa's face. He was quite right of course. You couldn't really argue with that.

"They still tread on thorns too, which sometimes go right through their shoes and prick their feet anyway," Nisa told them, "And then they go out and buy a new pair."

From that moment on, she would feel quite proud of not wearing shoes, while her dad translated what she'd said. They burst out laughing all over again, delighted by her last remark.

They asked if she had any questions for them in return, her

dad said. Nisa wanted to know about all the bits and bobs that hung from the straps they wore around their waists.

"And not much else besides," she'd noticed, but kept that thought to herself.

With her father translating, they told her about all the little tools they carried around with them, everywhere they went in the desert. Apart from an ostrich egg, one of which all of them had, none of them carried the same tools. They had no need to, for they shared everything.

The young man who'd asked her about shoes said something to the others, who all nodded. He untied something from his belt and offered it to Nisa, flat on the palms of his outstretched hands.

"What do I do?" she asked her father, afraid of making a mistake and offending him.

"You take it. It's a gift from them to you, Nisa," her dad proudly explained.

It was quite the longest, straightest thorn Nisa had ever seen, with a hole in the blunt end.

"Oh I get it. That's clever. It's a needle. A thorn made into a needle, like the thorns we were talking about together, that people sometimes tread on. Thank you," she said, with a rising feeling that a simple thank you wasn't quite enough. She looked to her father for help.

"Think about it, Nisa. That needle is an important tool out there in the desert, to him and the rest of them. They need it to sew all sorts of things together. Not just clothes and blankets, but bags and carriers, nets, leaves for shade or themselves even, if they get a cut. The whole group will have to go a long way to find a thorn bush like the one that came from, to replace it."

"And he'll have to drill the little hole in it too, which must take ages. Thank you so much, all of you. I'll treasure it," Nisa stood up and went to hug him. As soon as her dad nodded his permission, the young man wrapped his arms around her, patting her on the back and grinning from ear to ear. Without needing to be told further, Nisa went around the whole group and hugged each of them, in turn, to thank them all. For what was his, was all of theirs and they only had one needle between them, for that was all they needed. Yet he'd given it to her. They all had.

"But what can I give them in return? I want to, but I don't have anything important on me," Nisa looked to her father with pleading eyes. He smiled back and went on to explain.

"They don't work like that. They don't give in order to receive. If you tried, they might even be offended. It would lessen the meaning of their gift to you, in their eyes."

Back behind the market stalls, Cecily looked like she'd just seen a ghost. Staring dead ahead, she gripped Nisa's mum by the wrist.

"Ouch! Whatever's the matter?" she asked, raising her head to follow Cecily's gaze.

Two children were coming their way. One of them, a girl, swung a crooked stick, where once her leg had no doubt been. She was using it as a crutch, with the top nestled in her armpit.

The other, a boy about Nathi's age, had no legs at all. He shuffled along using both his arms as crutches, lifting his bottom off the floor, before plonking it down a little further on and lifting himself up with his arms again. Such was his only way of walking, if you could call it that. Both children were dressed in dirty, tattered rags and looked in dire need of a good meal and a bath.

Cecily went to grab the handles on the back of Nathi's chair, to pull him back, or turn him around, or wheel him away, anything, so he wouldn't see.

Nisa's mum barred her way, standing between them and staring into her friend's face.

"No, Cecily. Please don't. Let him see. Let him learn. Let him be."

When they looked down, Nathi seemed frozen, his hand half way up to his fixed face.

The children shuffled and hobbled closer until they saw him, sitting still in a chair with wheels on it, watching them. They stopped, to stare back at him.

Nisa's mum held her breath, holding Cecily together by her shoulders.

The girl leaned down to the boy, so they could whisper to each other. They came forwards.

"Hello," said Nathi, pleasantly, "Would you like to buy some fish?"

"We don't have any money to pay for it. Why's your chair got wheels on it?" the boy asked.

"Because my legs don't work. It helps me get around. Don't you have one?" he asked the boy.

The children chuckled shyly and looked at him like he must be mad.

"No we don't. Are you a prince or something? Because your chair looks like a throne."

"Nothing like. It's not a throne," Nathi was taken aback, that they could think such a thing.

"Your folks must be real rich though, for you to have a chair like that."

"No. My dad builds houses and gates and stuff for our village and others round about. That's all," Nathi told them, "What do your parents do?"

"Nathi! Don't be rude," Cecily snapped, knowing what their answer would most likely be.

"We don't have parents. We look after ourselves alright though. Pickings is good round here."

"Pickings? What do you mean?" asked Nathi.

"People leave all sorts of stuff behind. Stuff they can't sell. We eat that or sell it on, if we can."

"But it's only a weekly market, so what did you have for tea last night, or the night before?"

"Didn't have none, but we'll feast like a king and queen tonight, most likely."

"But where are your parents? What happened to them?" Nathi asked, clearly confused.

"He can't remember what happened to his. My leg got bitten off by a crocodile. The doctor sewed it up and stopped it bleeding. It hurt. He bandaged it up and wanted paying for it, but my folks didn't have the money, I reckon. All I know is, when I woke up they'd gone and I was left here. On my own, until he turned up," the girl shrugged, nodding down at her friend.

Nisa's mum covered her open mouth with her hand, while Cecily winced and looked away, as if she'd just been slapped in the face.

"And you have to get around like that, all the time?" asked Nathi, bluntly.

"Nathi! *Manners!*" Cecily hissed, turning back around.

"It's alright, Missus. He don't mean no harm by it. We know when people do. We get stuff thrown at us, or slapped round the back of the head mostly, by folks who mean us harm."

"But why would anyone mean you harm? What've you done wrong?" asked Nathi.

"Nothing, I swear! They don't want the likes of us around,

see?"

"Why not? I don't understand," Nathi scrunched up his face, utterly bewildered now.

"We reckon we makes them feel guilty, or we makes their place look untidy. And yes, by the way, of course this is how we get around, unless my stick snaps and then I have to hop for a while, until I find another one," the girl explained, as if it was all perfectly normal, to her.

Nathi realised that it was all perfectly normal, to her, which made him feel strangely sick.

"You can have my chair, if you'd like?" he offered, innocently.

"Whoa, son. Steady on there," Cecily interrupted, "I'm afraid they can't. How would you get around then, hmm? We can't afford another one, just like that."

"Oh sorry, I hadn't thought of that, but you'll have some fish at least?" he said to the children.

"I told you. We don't have no money," the little boy replied.

Nathi reached into his purse and grabbed a handful of coins, without counting it. He reached forward to give it to the boy, but realised that he couldn't hold his hands up, to collect it.

"Sorry, I didn't think," he muttered and gave it to the girl instead, "A barbel costs twelve, a perch costs nine and a catfish is six. What you pick is up to you, but you can keep the change," he told them, sounding very grown up, all of a sudden.

Both children beamed, looking back and forth from him to the pile of coins in her hand. To have a choice of what to buy and how much to spend was something they'd rarely known.

"And there's a special offer on today too," Nisa's mum added, as brightly as she could, "You get a free doughnut with every fish you buy. How about that? Can we tempt you?"

Wide-eyed, they sat down and counted up the coins,

whispering furiously to each another.

"Could I have a fine catfish, young man?" the little boy asked. The girl nudged him sharply with her elbow, "Please," he added, proudly.

Nathi took his money and wrapped up the biggest catfish he had.

"And could I trouble you for one of your best perch please?" the girl enquired, "Having never had the pleasure of tasting one before, you understand."

"Why yes of course, Madam. This looks like the best we have on sale, at the moment," Nathi answered, wrapping up a perch and taking the right money from her.

Nisa's mum handed the girl a bag with six doughnuts inside, as their extra special offer.

"Thank you kind Sir, Madam," the boy said, smiling up at them, with a sparkle in his eyes.

"It was a pleasure doing business with you, Sir. I hope we meet again, I do," the girl bowed.

"Any pleasure was all mine, I'm sure," Nathi replied, with a flourish of his hand.

The two of them hobbled away with their booty, their change and their dignity still in tact.

Nisa's mum squeezed Cecily's shoulders, both to comfort and congratulate her.

"Nathi, son, I'm so proud of you for doing that, like that. It breaks my heart and gladdens it, all at the same time," Cecily told him, with tears welling up in her eyes.

Nathi himself looked utterly lost, deep in twisting, tumbling thoughts.

The incredibly old woman reached out with both arms, beckoning Nisa to come closer. She looked to her dad, unsure what to do. When he nodded, she walked up to the Wise One, who laid her bony hands on Nisa's temples and closed her eyes, as if trying to read her mind.

"It's alright. She's what they call, "looking into you," her dad explained, "Another honour."

The old woman gripped the sides of her head quite tightly, until Nisa began to worry, a little. When she let go, her eyes snapped open really wide, as if staring into space. When at last she spoke in their clucking, clopping tongue, the rest of the group all bowed slightly, to Nisa!

Her father translated again, with his chest puffed out and his head held high.

"She says you are among people, as the ostrich is among the animals," he told her.

Nisa wasn't at all sure what to make of that, but thanked her anyway.

The incredibly old Wise One held her hand between the palms of her own and smiled at her warmly. She reached down and removed the ostrich egg from her skinny belt. With her head bowed, she held it out in her brittle hands, for Nisa.

"For me? To take it? Her ostrich egg? But that's the only way she can carry water in the desert, you said. So I can't," Nisa protested.

"Yet she's giving it to you, so that you may never be thirsty again. It means that she thinks your future is more important than hers. She's so very, very old, Nisa."

"I don't understand. How will she drink?" Nisa almost begged him.

"She won't," her father answered gravely, "Just take it."

"What, never again?" asked Nisa, turning the huge, smooth egg around in her hands.

"No, Nisa and that's enough questions now. Just work it out for yourself, quietly."

Nisa noticed that the young man who'd given her the needle, had tears in his eyes.

They said their solemn goodbyes and headed back to the hustle and bustle of the market.

Nisa did work it out for herself, carefully turning the ostrich egg over and over in her hands, like it was the most precious gift in the whole, wide world. She was brimming over with all sorts of questions about the Bushmen, but wisely chose to keep them to herself, for now.

By the time they got back to their stalls, Nathi had run right out of fish to sell. He sat there quietly, still trying to think things through.

Nisa sat down next to him, still turning the ostrich egg over and over in her small hands. The two children sat together in silence, with too much on their minds, for all of it to fit in.

"We haven't got much left now," her mum told her father, "Nearly done. We were just waiting for Joseph to come back, and you two. Did you have a nice time around the market?"

"We didn't get to see much. I'll tell you about it later," he whispered, nodding at Nisa.

"Oh bless her," her mother said. "Is she okay?"

"She's okay, honestly. Mighty fine, in fact," he recovered, straightening his back and smiling.

When Joseph came back, he couldn't believe how much money Nathi had made. They decided to go and look for something to buy with it. Before they set off, Cecily whispered a warning about "paupers" in Joseph's ear, but Nisa didn't know what that word meant. She didn't ask either.

While her parents packed up the stall around her, she turned the ostrich egg over and over in her slender hands, lost in the sad meaning of its shiny, round smoothness.

The incredibly brave old lady, the incredibly Wise One, knew she was about to die.

Nathi and Joseph came back with armfuls of new fishing rods, spool, hooks and tackle, a big bag full of all sorts of bits and bobs and a small tin bath, of all things!

"What the!" Cecily shrieked, "Didn't he want any toys or anything?"

"Only for Nisa," Joseph mouthed, pointing sideways at her, "He says he knows what he wants to do with it all, including the wheels and the tin bath. It's his money, after all," he shrugged.

"Wheels?" Nisa looked up and burst out laughing at Nathi, who looked pleased as Punch.

As their carts pulled away from the market; two small, pot-bellied children shuffled and hobbled out onto the road behind them, grinning and waving like mad.

Nathi waved back furiously, closely followed by Nisa, while he told her all about them. She went on to tell him about the gifts from her fellow Bushmen and what they meant.

A wicked grin slowly spread across her face, as she decided on the first thing she could do with her new needle; pricking both his thighs with it!

"OW! Ouch!" he yipped.

"Told you I'd get you back, twice!" she smiled, "And don't you give me 'ouch' because I know you couldn't feel it. You liar!"

"Am not! I just thought it would hurt more than it did," Nathi tried to defend himself.

He handed her a packet. Inside were three carved wooden animals, a crouching leopard, a fat hippopotamus and an ostrich, which jogged Nisa's memory. Yet more gifts for her to treasure.

"I never would've made a penny today, if it hadn't been for

you," he told her.

They played with her animals and chatted for much of the way home. Every so often, one of them would go quiet for a while, lost in thought, but the other would soon pull them out of it and have them laughing and squabbling, all over again.

When they were almost home, Nisa's curiosity finally got the better of her. Something had been bugging her. She decided it might be safe to ask her dad just one question, by now.

"Daddy? Why did the old lady, the Wise One, say I was an ostrich?" she risked.

"An ostrich!" Nathi pointed at her and burst out laughing.

"Many animals are drawn to the ostrich. Being so tall and black and white they can see him from miles away and head towards him. Having such good eyesight, he can see for miles around. Zebra can smell very well, while all the antelope hear very well. Once they all get together they can all relax, safe in the knowledge that no lions, hyenas or even Bushmen can get anywhere near them. One of them is bound to see or smell or hear them coming, but only whilst they're all gathered around an ostrich," he tried to explain, half over his shoulder.

"So if I'm an ostrich, Jasmine might be a zebra, say and the villagers are different antelope?"

"Exactly! Jasmine helps people in our village and we all feed her and fuss her, but we only know her and she only knows us, through you. So you're like an ostrich, helping other animals, to all help each other," he finished, relieved to be passing through the village gates.

"I'm not a silly antelope!" Nathi complained.

"You are too!"

Chapter Nine

In the hot, heavy days that followed, people began to wonder why it wasn't raining more. It hadn't much for this time of year, yet the river was still high.

They also began to wonder what Nathi was up to, bashing and twanging and clattering away in his own small work shed, whenever he had a spare moment. It turned out he'd made a cart out of the tin bath, with little wheels on it. He proudly towed it out behind his chair, folding his arms to a round of applause from his parents, Nisa and Alice.

Thabo looked on, wondering what was so clever about that. It looked stupid!

The next time he went fishing on the lake, Nathi had six rods cast out and floating on the water at any one time. He caught a whole lot of fish, way more than before, so it was just as well that his tin bath cart also floated, tied behind his canoe. He used it to hold all the fish he'd just caught, so he didn't have to come ashore until he'd caught enough. And when he did, he simply hitched it up to his chair and used it to cart all the fish home again, without getting his shorts all stinky.

He went out fishing with Jasmine, while she stuffed her face on water lilies and farted all the way home, or with his dad, or his mum, even Nisa's dad once, when nobody else could come. Nisa and Alice often went along too and kept each other company, while he was out on the lake.

Thabo wished he could go too, on his own though, which wasn't allowed. By now he was seething with jealousy over Nathi's success and spoiling to spoil his fun, once and for all.

In no time, Nathi had enough fish to take to market again,

a different market this time, and the next, and the next after that. He spent precious little of the money he made and had no idea what to do with it. Something would occur to him sooner or later, he said.

"Until such time it's yours to keep, if that's all you want to do with it," his dad advised him.

He always gave a fish or two to the boatman and he always bought Nisa a different carved animal, with an elephant, a zebra, a lion and an eland to add to her growing wooden zoo.

The children wilted in class, melting beneath the school's tin roof in the worst of the wet season's broiling, breathless heat. None of them could think straight about anything much, let alone lessons. Nobody really wanted to be there, not even the teacher, truth be told.

The screaming started quite suddenly, at the back of the class.

Nisa jumped up from her seat. Alice turned around sharply. Nathi spun round in his chair.

The dragleon's head shot up, out in the woods.

"It's all the children," she said to herself, swivelling her ears, "Coming from the school!"

By the time the dragleon got there, the playground was in utter chaos!

The teacher looked stunned, while the children were running about all over the place, most of them screaming still and some of them smacking at their feet, or stripping their clothes off!

"I didn't know what to do. I've never seen them before," the teacher warbled away at Jasmine, "All of a sudden they were everywhere, attacking us! Biting the children and everything," the teacher twitched nervously, "What're we going to do?"

"CHILDREN!" bellowed the dragleon, "COME here! All of you. Right now! That's it. Come on. Good. Now follow me.

Off we go, walking calmly away. That's all there is to it."

She made it sound so simple, leading the whole school up to the village square.

"That's what you should've done. Now what would be the sensible thing to do, from here?" Jasmine hissed out of the side of her mouth, inviting the teacher to take control of her class again. Gloria nodded and cleared her throat, to take up the reigns once more.

"Is everyone rid of them all? Pay attention Thabo! No more horrid little hangers-on?"

"No Miss," the children murmured, closely inspecting every inch of each other's clothing.

"Now class, your parents will be worried if they heard all that screaming. Alice! Thank you. So I want you all to go home, or to one of your parents where they work. Is that understood?"

"Yes Miss," came a general mumble.

"OW! You bully!"

"Thabo! Leave Alice alone!" the teacher barked, "Nisa! Don't you dare! Pardon? I don't care if he hit Alice first and don't you answer me back either. He didn't hit you, did he?" she carried on, "Now listen. They're only ants, when all is said and done. Whole swarms of them, granted, but you've all seen ants before, however huge these ones are," she shuddered, "So there's no need to be frightened any more now, is there?"

"No ,Miss," came another mumbled reply

"Off you go then and no dawdling. Thabo! Stop that at once, I said! That's the end of school for today, but do come back tomorrow, won't you?"

"Yes, Miss!" they answered, much more brightly.

"Well that cheered them up, at least" Jasmine whispered, as all but one child set off home.

When Nathi got back, he was told to wait in the middle of

the big puddle, by the front door.

"Probably the safest place for you right now. So don't move," his mum ordered. She dashed off to help an old lady she knew, without stopping to kiss his forehead, like she usually did.

Nisa got told to "Go and sit on your bed and stay there!" in the middle of the day, when she hadn't even been naughty!

Weirder still, the legs of her bed were standing in big bowls of water, which smelt funny. While her laundry basket was propped up against the head board, on the bed! Her parents had been in too much of a hurry to explain, rushing off to wherever instead.

The driver ants were coming though, sure enough, to invade the village in droves. Countless millions of them poured in through the streets like an occupying army, tickling into houses, raiding the shops, scouring the storage sheds and trickling into every nook and cranny they could find. All of a sudden, streams of big, black, biting ants seemed to be absolutely everywhere.

People tried to sweep them away, beat them back or fight them off, as best they could.

These ants fought back though, swarming in self defence. They seethed angrily up broom handles, clung viciously to flicking cloths, surged towards any swiping hands and surrounded stamping feet, determined to bite back! Soon the whole village was peppered with screams.

Only those old enough had ever seen driver ants before and knew what to do. The elders took to the streets, trying to convince people that they were a good thing, clearing the village of pests.

"If only everyone could please stop provoking them and above all, just STAY CALM!"

They didn't though. Most of the villagers panicked and

the ants declared all out war, it seemed. They massed around anyone trying to take them on, or stop them in any way, biting and forcing them back by sheer force of numbers. So the screaming continued as the ants carried on about their business, clearing the way for the plunder and slaughter of all the village vermin.

Countless tiny, frantic battles began, all over the village. Spiders, grasshoppers, cockroaches, beetles, wasps and butterflies, even Cecily's kitchen mice, it made no difference. Anything that couldn't get away got attacked. Smothered in ants and steadily butchered.

Ants had taken over the walls, the cupboards, the cracks and crevices. Behind this, under that, the eaves, thatched roofs, everywhere they could get into, inside people's houses.

Animals began barking, bleating and squawking all around the village, as tethered dogs or goats and all the cooped up chickens also came under attack.

"Oh no! Release your animals! Let them go!" the elders shouted, rushing around the streets to free whatever they could find. Others came outside to help, having given up indoors.

Nathi just sat there in his chair, safe in his puddle, trying to take it all in. He started to giggle.

Donkey and Jenny trotted down the lane towards him, stopped briefly for a fuss when they recognised him and trotted off again, to who knew where.

Villagers and elders hopped by or flapped past in ill-fitting sandals, their loose robes flying about around them. Goats and chickens tottered and scurried out of everyone's way, bleating or clucking in protest. While the yapping village dogs appeared to be thoroughly enjoying themselves, chasing after anyone who ran past, yipping and nipping at their heels.

Thabo was busy flicking ants at people with a long stick.

Nathi saw him punch the air, when one of his missiles hit home and bit the teacher, who screamed on the spot like an opera singer.

Driver ants squeezed in around the hated boards over Nisa's window. They tickled in through the tiniest of cracks or ran down the walls from the thatched roof. They seethed in through her bedroom door in streams that split and parted, spreading out across the floor.

Nisa realised why her laundry basket had been put on her bed; to save the snake inside it!

Ants were trickling into, onto, under everything. Except her bed, she noticed. Looking down, she could see them reaching the edge of the water in the bowls and turning back. They wouldn't cross to climb up and attack her. The thought of it made her skin prickle.

Suddenly she SCREAMED! Really SCREAMED!

At the scorpion, THERE!

Having dropped down from its hole in the wall, wriggling and jiggling, it scuttled and scrabbled across the floor, snipping their heads off and stabbing at the ants all around it. More and more of them seethed towards it though, blundering into its squirming struggles. They hung on to its flailing tail, swarmed up its kicking legs, even hanging on to its wicked pincers, anything to weigh it down. Still more ants piled onto the scorpion, biting and clinging on. It thrashed about, frenzied, desperate to be rid of them.

Nisa realised the ants were winning! She found herself willing them on, while she watched.

Soon they'd covered the scorpion completely, writhing all over it in a heaving mass. Its frantic struggles began to fade and falter. It wriggled more slowly and kicked more feebly. Its tail no longer struck out, as it weakened under their sheer weight of numbers.

Then the butchery began.

Nisa leaned forward to watch in horror, as first one foot came away and then another.

A big soldier sawed through a joint, higher up one of the scorpion's legs. A couple of workers straddled the piece without fuss or feeling and carted it off, back the way they'd come, through the door. It was soon followed by the dreaded stinger, the rest of the legs and the tail, all in sections, neatly sawed off at the joints, as if the ants knew exactly what they were doing.

Still the scorpion squirmed in vain beneath the seething ants, after all its legs had gone!

As it slowly rolled over, some of the soldiers hooked their jaws in between the segments on its tummy. Nisa could see them slicing along the edge of the broad scales, bit by bit, like living can openers. Gooey scorpion innards spilled out onto their heads. Even that was gathered up in mouthfuls and taken away. She pulled a face as the scorpion stopped its pitiful writhing at last.

The ants continued to saw their way through its hard shell. Piece by piece simply removed, until even its head had been broken up and carted off, in bite-size bits.

All of a sudden there was nothing left of the scorpion that had haunted her room, where just a moment before, there'd been a furious struggle of life and death.

Something occurred to Nisa. Her head snapped up, away from the carnage on the floor. She scanned the walls and there! A ball of ants seethed around the clothes hook, right where the praying mantis liked to sit, watching over her for hours on end.

"Oh no! Daddy! DADDY! DADDY!" Nisa screamed and screamed and screamed again.

Nathi tried to spin his wheels, but they'd sunk and stuck

fast in the mud. He shouted for Jasmine, bent double, pushing and pulling and practically turning purple, but still stuck fast.

Jasmine hurtled past him, thundering up to Nisa's window and cursing the boards still over it. Nisa was wailing inside though. She couldn't stand by and do nothing. So she wrenched the planks aside and stuck her head in through the window.

"They're killing our mantis!" howled Nisa, "I can't see her eggs either. They've taken them!"

Jasmine couldn't reach in to lift her outside, much as she wanted to, but her best friend was in tears! She had to do something. Looking around the small, enclosed room, she decided to give something a try. Breathing out as hard and fast as she could, the dragleon huffed until her lungs felt like they'd collapse and puffed until she went cross-eyed. She really did turn purple.

She tried to think of happy thoughts throughout, but found herself remembering what the fisherman had said, about seeing her dancing through the streets with everyone. True, she'd rarely felt any happier, but the end result was truly bizarre, even by her standards.

The driver ants stopped what they were doing and appeared to be shuffling into rows, right across the bedroom floor. They all stood upright and . . .

"Ooh! Did they all clap, just then? What on earth have you done, Jasmine?" Nisa wondered.

"I'm not sure, but I think, yes. They definitely all jumped to the left and took a step to the right then and oh dear!" the dragleon gulped, "Who knew ants even had hips, to put their hands on?"

They went on to kick forwards with their little anty feet and clapped again, all at once!

Nisa squealed. She couldn't quite believe her eyes, but

they were. There was no doubt about it. The driver ants were dancing! She was dumbfounded and delighted, all at the same time.

As the two of them watched, the ants began to shuffle and strut and spin and hitch, kicking their teeny legs out, all of them together, in lines. They clapped their little anty hands again.

"If you listen closely, you can actually hear it when they clap! It's incredible!"

The ants began trying more difficult moves and linking them together. They even appeared to be getting cocky, once they got the hang of coasters, rocking chairs, mambo and scissor steps.

Their timing was absolutely ant perfect. They seemed to be really enjoying their tiny selves.

Nisa and Jasmine looked at each other for a moment, scarcely able to believe it. They both began to smile and giggle, as Nisa began to move.

Whatever the sweet scented messages carried on the dragleon's breath, they'd been picked up by the ants in the confines of Nisa's room, passed on through their ranks as countless, tiny smelly signals and sent from one ant to the next, right down the lines and right outside the door, Jasmine noticed. She wondered, pulling her head back through the window to see what was going on outside. The first thing she saw was Nisa's parents, standing open-mouthed.

Next she saw Nathi, giggling his head off while everyone else in the street stood still, looking shocked. Only then did she notice what the ants were doing, right down the lane and beyond.

They were dancing in rows, all of them. Kick, slide, step to the right.

Perfectly in time, in step with each other. Back, turn, step to the left.

They were emptying out of houses, sheds and shops. Spin, step, sideways. Clap!

To join those already dancing through the streets. Jazz hands, shuffle, two steps more.

Slowly but surely, they were heading out of town. And . . . wiggle those little ant bottoms!

People lined the streets, staring in amazement. Where once they'd tried to stomp on the warring ants; now they watched where they put their feet. Every time the ants did a little clap, or wiggled their little ant bottoms like that, the villagers started to giggle. They couldn't help it. Laughter replaced the screaming of moments before, as the driver ants line danced their way out of town. Bow, step, forwards, kick!

People bent down to get a really good look. Some even knelt down, lowering their faces to the ground, as if needing absolute proof that their eyes weren't deceiving them. Or their ears!

"Ha! Even the ones carrying things do what moves they can. Look!" one man shouted.

"Hee Hee! You can hear it when they all stomp their teeny feet, like that!"

"There's three of 'em carrying the same bit here and even they're doing some of the steps!"

On and on the ants danced, to everyone's disbelief and delight. Clap! Nod, link arms, spin.

With everyone so distracted, Thabo sauntered to the edge of town, unnoticed. He slipped out through the gate and soon broke into a run along the lake road, well on his way to causing more trouble, than even he had thought possible.

Suddenly there was a scream of laughter, coming from Nisa's room. Jasmine stuck her head back through the window, to see what else could be so funny. Nisa was standing on her

119

bed, moving her own hips and staring into the open laundry basket, which rocked from side to side.

"He is! Even the snake's trying to do it, without any arms or legs!" she squealed.

"Oh go on. Tip him out. Let's see," begged the dragleon, "The ants have all left in here. They're half way up the street by now, so he'll be perfectly safe on the floor."

Sure enough, when Nisa tipped the house snake onto her bedroom floor, he shuffled to one side, looped forwards, bowed down and turned around. He even looked frustrated when the ants all clapped outside, since he couldn't quite join in.

The two of them howled with laughter at his antics, until Jasmine stopped to stare at Nisa.

The little girl stepped back, kicked, turned, shuffled and stepped forwards, without realising she was doing it! Not until she clapped her hands together did she notice Jasmine staring at her. She screamed with laughter all over again. Only this time, at herself!

"Um, I think you'd better come outside, for a breath of fresh air," Jasmine suggested, once she'd recovered from another fit of the giggles, "Besides, they're leaving and you really don't want to miss this. It's quite something. I'm rather proud of it, to tell you the truth. Come on."

Nisa joined everyone else as they slowly followed the ants, line dancing their way out of town.

Two steps forward, sideways shuffle, onto your heel and turn.

A few people gave her funny looks when she stuck out her bottom and gave it a little wiggle, right along with the ants. Some began to join in though, laughing out loud as they did so. More and more people began to copy the line dancing ants, hopelessly out of time, but thoroughly enjoying themselves anyway. Turn, step forwards, jump and clap!

Half the village clapped right along with them, that time, followed by a ragged cheer.

Rarely could anyone remember having so much fun. This was even better than the well behaved monkeys had been, tidying up the mess they'd made as they left the village for good.

Hands on hips, kick, step forwards, little anty jazz hands, shimmy and clap! "HOORAY!"

Two steps further, turn and . . . bow.

When the massed ranks of driver ants reached the very outskirts of town, they got back down on all sixes and headed off to their new nest, wherever that may be.

A huge cheer went up. Everyone congratulated Jasmine, their very own magical dragleon!

People headed home in dribs and drabs, smiling and joking about what had just happened. They'd be talking about it for weeks to come. After all, it wasn't every day you saw the like.

"Yes, I'm still here! Thank you for not caring," Nathi grumbled at his approaching father.

Joseph pushed him out of the muddy puddle, picked up the bucket they kept by the front door and sloshed water over the chair's wheels, to wash the mud off before Nathi went indoors.

Nisa sat on her bed, suddenly feeling sad as she remembered what happened to the mantis and her beautiful egg cases. They were gone, just like that, for ever more.

Her father came in and sat on the bed next to her, asking what the matter was. While she explained, he put his arm around her and pulled her to his side.

"Our mantis would soon have faded and died anyway, having laid all her eggs. Your snake survived though! Let's not forget that," he brightened suddenly, "And I'll bet there's no more scorpion for you to worry about now, is there? They killed that too, hmm?"

"Yes and I watched! It was horrid in a way, but I'm glad to be rid of it," Nisa admitted.

"Right, let's get your bed back into its corner, shall we?" he said, lifting it out of the bowls of water, "First one end," he grunted and let it thump back down onto the floor, "And then the other," he bumped her down again and pushed the bed back against the wall, with her still sitting on it, which cheered her up some.

"Oh and I've got a little present for you," he smiled, reaching into a stiff pouch on his hip. From it, he produced two perfectly formed praying mantis egg cases, "I had time to save them."

She took them carefully in her cupped hands, able to look at them closely for the first time.

"They're beautiful, so delicate and . . . and intricate. Is that the right word, Daddy?"

"That is a perfect word, Nisa. Take care of them, won't you? Maybe you'll see them hatch soon. It's like a little miracle, when they do. You'll see," he said, kissing her on the forehead.

Someone began pounding on the front door. Nisa nearly jumped out of her skin!

"Alright, alright! You'll hammer it off its hinges!" her dad shouted, getting up to open it.

Chapter Ten

"Thabo! Have you seen Thabo? We can't find him anywhere. He's disappeared! Gloria said she told all the children to go home when the ants came, but he never showed up. She should've walked him home, so it's her fault and I told her so, but has Nisa seen him? Can you ask her?" his mother stopped, but only to draw breath, before carrying on.

"Nathi hasn't. I already asked him. Well, not since he claims he saw him flicking ants at people, which I don't believe for an instant," she scowled.

Nisa hadn't seen him, but pointed out that she'd never known Nathi to lie about anything.

"And Miss did tell us all to go home. Everyone else did, so it's hardly her fault if . . ."

"I didn't ask for your opinion, child! Only if you'd seen my Thabo," his mum cut her short.

Nisa's dad squeezed the top of her shoulder tightly, warning her not to answer back.

"The poor woman seemed worried sick," he explained with some feeling, after she'd gone.

His parents knocked from door to door around the entire village, but nobody had seen Thabo. He never was one do as he was told though, or be where he was supposed to be, to put it politely. Everyone knew it, so nobody was surprised. They'd all heard tales or seen him up to no good, so nobody took too much notice. Had it been a more trustworthy child, they might have acted sooner.

Nisa slept the sleep of someone finally free of monsters living under their bed.

The following day, her parents decided to risk the muddy

road to a distant market. They were up at the crack of dawn, when Nisa discovered that her snake had gone.

"He's not in his basket and he didn't come into my bed last night either," she wailed.

"I don't like the thought of him in your bed anyway, but he probably went off hunting. He hasn't eaten for days, but you gave him such a nice home, I'm sure he'll be back," her dad said.

Sally next door screamed and dropped a big cooking pot, by the sound of it, which rolled around on the floor. Nisa's mum rushed round to see what the matter was.

"Nisa! Get in here, will you?" she shouted through the walls.

Nisa did so, wondering what she'd done now.

"It seems your snake decided on a little sleepover," her mum told her, with one eyebrow raised, "Because Sally here, got quite a shock when she picked up her best copper pot. Hmm?"

"Coiled up inside it! Thanks to your snake, it's dented now. Look at it!" Sally complained.

"Sorry Sally," Nisa muttered, but felt like pointing out that it was Sally who'd dropped her precious pot and not her, "Did you see which way he went, so I can try and catch him?"

"Out the door! As far away as possible, I hope," Sally replied, tapping her foot.

Nisa looked, but couldn't find him anywhere, before she went to school.

Her parents took both carts to market. They were in for a back-breaking day, as it turned out. The cart wheels stuck in the mud, twice on the way there and once on the way back, as if to add insult to injury. Digging them out had been hard work. So they were late getting home and both flopped down into their chairs, exhausted.

Nisa ran to tend the donkeys, praying her parents had been too tired to talk to anyone, on their way in. It had been an eventful day in the village, whilst they'd been away at the market. They were bound to find out about it sooner or later, even though it was hardly her fault, despite what everyone said. She was bound to be in big trouble unless perhaps, she told them herself before anyone else got to them. Nisa gulped, reaching a brave decision.

As soon as she got back to the house, she told them everything, as best she could and from what she'd heard, mostly from people who'd been wagging their fingers and shouting at her.

It began when the new chicken coop all but exploded, with squawking chickens rocketing into the air. They landed wherever like feathery bombs, darting about in a mad panic, tottering every which way, fluttering and clucking this way and that and getting under everyone's feet.

"Nisa's snake got in the hen house! The cobra killer! There he goes!" somebody shouted.

People tried to herd the terrified chickens back towards their coop, but they wouldn't go anywhere near it, let alone back inside through the wide open gate. Stupid birds!

There was only one thing for it. The villagers had to catch them, charging around after charging chickens, crashing into each other and collapsing in a heap. Half the village was in uproar, dashing after dodging hens, diving at them as they squawked and scattered, tripping up to fall flat on their faces, grazing their hands and knees. One by one though, chicken by flapping chicken, the villagers managed to clear the streets.

Even the pesky cockerels got cornered and caught in the end, but put up a fight first, pecking and kicking at anyone who grabbed at them.

Until somebody finally managed to lunge at the very last bird, rolled over and came back up with it, holding it aloft in triumph.

Once the fuss had finally died down, the villagers counted their chickens, several times.

They were not happy. Two plump chicks had gone missing alright and everyone knew where!

The bulging snake wanted peace and quiet, somewhere safe to digest his double meal. He settled for a nice big basket, full of comfy laundry. He was used to laundry baskets, after all.

Suddenly, he was bobbing up and down inside his new basket, hoisted upwards and rudely thrust into broad daylight. He found himself somehow suspended, it felt like, which was not where he wanted to be. When his coils began to slip and slide, he realised he was falling! Out through one leg, of a pair of frilly bloomers!

Rearing up, he got his chin hooked over the washing line. He managed to haul himself up, but found he had nowhere to go. He stretched out, swaying in the sunshine, only to find himself face to flushed face with the washer woman, who was screaming her head off!

She fell over backwards, her outstretched hams of arms catching the clothes lines behind her, which snapped with a loud twang! Knickers and bloomers, pants and smalls, half the village's underwear, pinged off the line and sailed up into the air. It floated high above the streets for a moment, before slowly drifting back down, landing mostly where it shouldn't.

The washer woman stood up with some difficulty, looked around and screamed all over again. To her horror, several confused goats were busy deciding if underwear might be tasty. Dogs were off and away with it, playing tug of war or chase, while several villagers threw other people's under garments at her, not wanting to wear them as hats.

"Well at least they were clean!" she'd shouted back at them, bending down to pluck laundry out of, "Just about every muddy puddle it could possibly have landed in!" she wailed.

Quite forgotten amidst the chaos and still wearing his frilly, flying bloomers, the house snake sailed through the air, to land on a nearby roof with a soft thud.

He'd had quite enough excitement for one day and buried his head in the thatch, like an ostrich burying its head in the sand, when things all got a bit too much for it.

Later on, a young man climbed up a ladder to start work on a thatched roof. The first thing he noticed, and you really couldn't fail to notice them, was one enormous pair of frilly bloomers!

"Whose are these, then? Eh?" he yelled to anyone listening, waving said bloomers about on a stick, for everyone to laugh at. They did laugh too, but the joke would soon be on him. He was about to get the fright of his life and an unexpected bath!

Reaching to one side, he went to pull out what looked like a charred stick. As soon as he gripped it, the other end burst from the thatch, whipping around to strike at his face.

It missed, but he fell over backwards, off the ladder and down into a water trough. He landed with an almighty SPLASH and a few choice swear words, ending in "Girl's damn snake!"

"Fetch Nisa!" shouted the thatched roof's owner.

"She'll be in school though," his wife had pointed out.

"I don't care if she's in school!" he yelled, "Get her out of it and up here now! She can re-fill our water trough, for a start. It's half empty now, thanks to this baboon!"

"Who're you calling a baboon? Oh and it's alright, by the

way. Thank you for not asking, but I don't think I'm hurt," the roofer had complained.

"Yes. Right! That's quite enough of all this nonsense! Someone has to catch that snake. Fetch Nisa this instant! I agree!" a passing elder had bellowed.

"But you can't send a child up a ladder, surely?" Sally, she was told, had objected.

"I'll give her 'up a ladder', I'll throw her up there!" the roofer bawled.

Somebody started to laugh as he slopped water everywhere, getting out of the water trough.

"It's not funny!" he shouted, but it looked funny to everyone else.

"Then summon the dragleon!" the elder had bawled, "She can reach up there, I'm sure."

"Will you listen to him? Who do you think you are? Don't you mean, 'Could someone please ask Jasmine nicely, if she could possibly give us a hand?' She doesn't have to, you know," the wife had corrected him.

"Madam! One of your elders is who I am. Right! You there!" he'd bawled, pointing at an innocent passer-by, who wished he hadn't been.

"Go and fetch Nisa from school. Tell Gloria I said so. Then go and find Jasmine to ask her, very politely mind, if she could possibly help us?" the elder had sneered.

As it happened, Jasmine was walking up to wait for Nisa at the school gate. It was lunch time, when the call came for Nisa to drop everything and get to the village square.

"Oh and could you possibly please come too, to lend a hand? I mean a talon," the runner begged Jasmine, as politely as he could, "Um, sharpish like," he added, rather spoiling things.

The two of them looked at each other, while the runner

128

explained what all the fuss was about.

"Oh good. Somebody found him. I hope he's alright," Nisa brightened up instantly.

"Um, I wouldn't say 'good' if I were you. Not to anyone with chickens, or laundry."

"What a lot of fuss over a harmless little house snake," Jasmine scoffed.

"Um. He's not that little to us. He must be six feet long," the young man pointed out.

People had scowled at Nisa as she made her way through the village. Very few of them actually said anything because the dragleon walked beside her, so they didn't dare. Their bitter silence spoke volumes though and Nisa began to worry.

When they reached the scene of the snake's latest crime, the thatched roof's owner, the wet roofer and several village elders gave Nisa a good telling off, wagging their fingers at her.

A few kind people stood up for her though.

"Anyone would think she'd done all this herself!" the runner had pointed out.

"Steady on. She's only a little girl," another objected, "Blimey! They are big bloomers."

"You didn't mind her snake when it killed that cobra!" even Sally sprang to her defence.

"ENOUGH! You've all had your say. Now let's just do something about it, shall we? I'll take the snake as far away as possible and set it free, if only I can catch it," Jasmine proposed, turning around and raising her long neck, to look over the thatched roof.

Somebody fetched a big chest that locked, which Sally lined with the monstrous bloomers.

"Well? We know he likes them," she shrugged, which made people chuckle.

Jasmine began to lift the thatch up, carefully, bit by bit, working her way along the wall until suddenly; she froze, signalling for the box to be brought forward. She reached up slowly with her free hand and . . . suddenly thrust it under the thatch.

"Got him!" she shouted in triumph, at which everyone cheered, all too briefly.

In the cramped space beneath the thatched eaves, the poor snake was suddenly terrified. He found himself gripped by a scaly monster, with talons! Of course he bit it, what else could he do? Except wish he was a spitting cobra, which could really defend itself!

"OW! That hurt. I think he got one of my scales," Jasmine complained, pulling the snake out.

One of her scales had indeed stuck in the snake's mouth, until he managed to swallow it down, with some difficulty. Straight away, Jasmine's whole body began to pulse with fantastic rainbow colours, as she looked down at the crowd. She expected a round of applause at least, but instead they stood there in silence, gawping at her unexpected waves of colour.

All of a sudden, the humble house snake must've felt very strange indeed. He hissed and threw a vengeful coil around the dragleon's wrist. Even snakes can have a wish come true, it turned out, thanks to the dragleon's magical scales. What was once a harmless house snake now spread out its hood and reared up in her grasp, willing her to face him.

"Jasmine! Look out!" Nisa screeched, "Your colours! He swallowed your scale! Let go!"

Jasmine stopped changing colours and looked back at the snake in her hand. He must've made a wish and changed, she realised to her horror! She no longer had hold of a house snake. She was holding a spitting cobra!

Quick as a flash, the gaping snake spat, straight at her face! Two jets of venom splashed into her eyes, which began to burn, instantly.

Jasmine howled and dropped the snake, which landed in the open box, thankfully.

Before anyone could hurt him, Nisa rushed to close the lid, but it took what seemed like ages to pull it all the way up and over. For a moment she stared into the cobra's steely eyes. He stared straight back at her, until the lid thumped shut. She could've sworn she saw something there. He could so easily have spat at her, right into her eyes. Yet he hadn't. Had he somehow recognised her and held back, even as a spitting cobra? She liked to think so. He was her friend, after all.

"She picked up a cobra! Not my snake at all," Nisa lied quickly and loudly to everyone, "It can't have been. You all saw! And you made her do it!" she shouted, pointing at the elders.

Nisa reckoned she just about got away with it, judging by the worried looks on their faces.

Jasmine started rubbing at her eyes, furiously. Her petal scales, normally so pretty, spiked out into black thorns. The ground shook as she hopped backwards, nearly squashing them all.

People began to realise the danger, as the dragleon whirled around in pain. Her tail smacked into a wall, in an explosion of sticks and crumbling mud.

"The water trough! Quick man, grab a bucket!" one of the elders ordered.

The roofer dunked a bucket into the water trough. Jasmine nearly knocked him into it again! She spun round on the spot, moaning and rubbing her eyes. He waited to fling the water up at her face, but it sloshed up her nostrils and into her mouth, as much as into her eyes.

"Sorry Jasmine. Hold still for a second," he asked, scooping out another bucket of water.

The dragleon began to panic. The burning in her eyes got worse. She couldn't hold still.

"I hurts! It hurts!" she wailed, stamping her foot and smashing the trough to smithereens. Water sloshed everywhere, but where it was needed. It gushed down the street in a sheet as she stamped up and down, paddling on the spot in stinging frustration.

"Get her out of here! Before she has the whole damn village down!" another elder shouted.

"Jasmine. JASMINE! It's me!" Nisa yelled, "Calm down. We have to flush your eyes out, but you're going to have to stay still and let us do it. Do you hear me?" Nisa begged her.

She tried. Standing still for a second while a scream rose up from somewhere inside her, clenching her fists and grinding her teeth, growling at the searing pain.

"Open your eyes. Now!"

"I can't. I CAN'T!" she screamed, wincing as she struggled to lift her eyelids.

SPLASH! The water hit her, right in the face. She had to stop herself from smacking the poor roofer and then the world went black, but her eyes were open. All of a sudden. Just. Black!

"I can't see at all now! I CAN'T SEE!" she screamed, so loudly that the whole village stopped. Flailing her talons around in front of her, the dragleon half turned, ripping great clods off the top of the wall and scattering thatch, all over the place. She turned and started to run, straight into another wall. She only stopped when it toppled in front of her, in a rumbling cloud of dust.

"Jasmine PLEASE! Follow me. Follow my voice. The river's not far. Come on," Nisa yelled.

She ran a little way ahead, calling to the stumbling dragleon, still flailing her arms out in front of her face. She swiped a lean-to by accident, flinging it across the street behind her. It knocked poor Sally off her feet. She got up, gasping for breath, winded, but otherwise unhurt.

"Calm down. Come on, Jasmine. You can do it," Nisa encouraged her, running on ahead.

The pain seared up behind Jasmine's eyes again. She whipped around as if to face it, smashing a pole as she did so. The shop porch caved in, scattering boxes of bouncing fruit across the street.

"This way! This way! Turn to face my voice. That's it, now. Come on," Nisa called.

As Jasmine bumbled blindly towards the little voice, people came out to watch. They started shouting, louder and louder, until Jasmine could no longer hear Nisa's voice. She lurched to her left, threatening to trample people, who all crushed backwards down an alleyway.

The elders bellowed for quiet after that, so the desperate dragleon could follow Nisa, her Nisa, like a light in her darkness, a little ray of hope, she said later.

Each time the stinging spiked behind her eyes, Jasmine threw up her head and turned off course, unable to stand it a moment longer. Another wall came crashing down, a porch, some tools, neatly stacked, clattered and scattered, thorn trees sprouted, a cooking pot kicked across the street, clonking. Each time she would hear Nisa's voice come back to her, urging her to follow, which she did. At least she tried, she really did, but every so often, her eyes would scream at her from inside her head and she simply couldn't stand it. More thorn bushes burst up behind her.

She growled and flailed her arms, or flapped her hands as she whipped around or stamped her feet, anything to fight the terrible, blinding pain. A ragged line of growing thorns followed in her wake, threading through the middle of the village.

"Try all fours, Jasmine! Drop down. Trust me. We're getting there. All fours!" Nisa bawled.

The dragleon heard her and tried it and knew she was right, the moment she tried it. So long as she followed that brave little voice, it was safer this way. It was. She could do it.

Everyone gasped when she nearly squashed a puppy, which cowered, confused, in a corner. Its mother ran out to collect it, barking furiously at Jasmine, who managed to say she was sorry.

She left a trail of destruction and spiking thorn trees, thrusting up as saplings in her wake, until finally, Nisa got her out through the gates and off towards the river. Everyone had cheered!

Poor Jasmine smashed through a thorn tree, one of her own, flinging squirrels into the grass. Nisa didn't mind because she never liked it there anyway, where Jasmine had once roared at the villagers. She let out a rising scream and started to run, anything to reach the river.

It felt better, pounding along on all fours like a living earthquake, taking it out on the ground beneath her feet, flattening her own jasmine bushes.

Nisa dodged out of the way, screaming at her side as she thundered past, gathering pace, pounding the ground, quicker and faster and faster still, until the dragleon took off!

"Straight ahead! Run. Yes! You're almost there. Keep running! You're FLYING, Jasmine! FLY!" Nisa cheered, punching the air as the dragleon's stubby wings lifted her clear off the ground. She swept through the air like a thunder cloud, storming over the fields, the wind howling in her face. Jasmine opened her eyes. She had to. She couldn't help it. She was FLYING!

Yet still she couldn't see, which shocked her all over again and down she tumbled, straight into the river, with one almighty SPLASH!

Nisa was jumping up and down on the track, punching the air and whooping with joy.

Jasmine rolled around in the river, making waves. She thrashed her head from side to side in the choppy water, washing the venom from her eyes, splashing her face and blinking.

She'd stopped screaming at least as Nisa rushed up to the river bank and finally, the dragleon stopped thrashing about as well. She risked opening her big, bloodshot eyes, blinking madly.

They were sore, very sore, but she could see daylight and make out a dark line, the tops of distant trees. The bare fields came blinking back into view, the river and the village in the distance.

"And there I was, waving up at her. The most welcome sight she said she'd ever seen. But she flew Mum, Dad, she really flew!" Nisa finished explaining everything, with a sigh.

"Don't use words like "damn" in future. Even if someone else has," was all her dad said.

"But aren't you cross with me? Nearly everyone else was," Nisa admitted.

"What for?" her dad shrugged, much to Nisa's surprise.

"Seems to me that you did very well. You couldn't help telling everyone a lie, *for once,* mind, because you were trying to save Jasmine's skin. I think that's allowed. You also saved the village from far more damage and you told your tale very well too, I might add. So well done," her mum said, seeming quite proud of her!

"But all the damage and everything. The chickens and the

laundry? I told you."

"The snake and Jasmine did that. Not you!" her dad decided, "They can hardly blame a snake for being a snake, or Jasmine either. They only have themselves to blame for, for asking her into the village in the first place and, and, and making her pick up a . . . spitting cobra, of all things! They should be ashamed of themselves. I'll say so too at the village meeting," he bristled for a moment, before cringing and daring to ask, "Um. Is he still a cobra though, or will it wear off?"

"What I wished for hasn't and that was ages ago," Nisa lowered her gaze and admitted, which surprised her parents. She never normally talked about whatever happened, *that* day.

There was a long pause, while her dad nodded his head slowly, thinking things through.

Nisa had told her parents about making a wish, with Jasmine, but they hadn't believed her at the time. Only now they weren't so sure. They could even guess what their daughter had wished for, but she'd explained right from the outset that if she ever told them, it might stop her wish from working. Since that was the last thing they wanted, they'd agreed not to risk asking her about it and they never had either, much to Nisa's relief.

"So where is he now, the snake?" her dad asked, choosing his words very carefully.

"Jasmine's taken him back to the woods, as far away as she can before she has to go to sleep. She gets very tired, granting wishes. Even weird accident wishes for snakes I should think, but I won't see him again now," Nisa slumped a little, "And he liked me. He must have. Even as a cobra he remembered me. He didn't spit when he could have and it made me feel, oh I don't know, somehow special," she said, hoping her snake was okay, out there in the wild, with her dragleon.

"Make no mistake, my girl. You are very special indeed," her mum said, giving her a hug.

It wasn't a school day, on account of the teacher being needed at the village meeting.

Nisa, Alice and Nathi had arranged to go fishing with the dragleon.

Her eyes weren't stinging so much, after a good long sleep and much more rinsing in cold water. She waved at them now across the sunny clearing, as the children rushed to greet her.

Scooping the girls up into her arms, a spray of flowers splashed up all around Jasmine.

Nathi trundled right through them, reaching up for his hug at the last moment. Even more flowers popped up, half of which he mowed down as they left, heading back towards the village. They'd soon bounce right back up again, a bit like Nathi himself, from time to time.

There was something Jasmine had to do first, before they all went fishing. People were finding it difficult to walk through the village, on account of all the spreading thorn trees.

Hanging her head, Jasmine put up with their filthy looks, whilst walking from one thorn tree to the next down the main street, laying her talons on them and dissolving them where they stood.

Nathi was delighted, following on behind and scraping up piles of the wibbly-wobbly black bits with a shovel. He heaped it into his tin bath cart, to use as fish bait later on.

"Ooh. Hang on there, Nisa isn't it? I've been looking out for you," the shop keeper who she'd given a piece of her mind to called over, "Here, please accept this as a gift from the shop. I saved it for you, seeing as you liked it," he said, kindly offering her the doll he'd dropped.

"Thank you. I wasn't expecting that. It's very good of you," Nisa accepted his dolly apology. He'd even cleaned her dress, she noticed, while the others wondered what that was all about and since when had Nisa ever liked dolls? She told them, just as soon as they were out of earshot.

Having cleared the streets and put up with people making comments, some of which were surprisingly kind, asking how her eyes were today or how she was feeling now, Jasmine and the children set off towards the fishing lake, much to her relief.

As soon as they were out of sight, Nisa handed the doll to Alice, if she wanted it?

"Why do they always make dolls with such big eyes? It's silly," Nisa scoffed.

"Thank you, but it's a good job you've got such big eyes Jasmine, or you'd probably still be blind," Alice said, "I'm sure we would be, maybe for ever, if a cobra spat at one of us."

"So the bigger your eyes are, the safer you'll be from spitty cobras," Nathi reasoned.

After that, the children tried to make their eyes look as big as possible, giggling as they stared at each other. They walked along, looking like they were surprised, until it made their eyes ache.

Suddenly they stopped, having all smelt it, as clear as toffee popcorn. The children huddled closer to Jasmine, who could smell something very dead as well, but kept that to herself.

Turning her head from side to side, she worked out where the leopard was, in through the trees.

"Do excuse me and please don't be scared of me, will you?" she warned them, before working up to a blood-curdling GGGRRROWL, warning the leopard to keep its distance, or else!

"I think we'll come back home along the river road, don't you?" she suggested brightly.

They hurried on to the lake, where Nathi couldn't wait to get out on the water, while Jasmine couldn't wait to get started on the water lilies.

Every fish he landed earned Nathi a cheer from Nisa, Alice and sometimes Jasmine too, when her mouth wasn't full. Every fish he landed earned him a bit more money too, but no matter how hard they pressed him, he couldn't tell them what he planned to do with it all. He didn't know himself. Something would occur to him sooner or later, was all he could say.

Thanks largely to his fishing success, the others had seen Nathi's confidence growing, day by day. They were happy to play their part in it, while he began to feel like he could do anything he wanted, so long as he put his mind to it. However, there was one thing that he wanted to do more than anything else in the whole wide world, which would soon land him in serious trouble.

Jasmine had eaten far too many water lilies again. The mass of fragrant bubbles popping on the lake's surface gave her away. The children began to giggle, but Nathi soon stopped laughing.

"I wish you wouldn't do that! It does something silly to the fish. They've stopped biting again, just like the last time you did it," he complained bitterly.

He came ashore in something of a sulk, throwing his rods down in disgust.

So they sat watching dragonflies and damselflies flitting about and glinting in the sunshine. As if speaking a language all their own, made of dipping, darting movements and the play of light on delicate wings and tiny, shiny, metal scales.

The children made up what they might be saying to each other, sometimes shouting, sometimes whispering, sometimes gossiping, or even flirting and sometimes just singing in the sunlight.

It was enough to cheer anyone up. Perhaps the grown-ups should've tried it, but instead they made their way towards the dreaded village meeting house.

It was going to be a long one, everyone knew. The elders had warned them all in advance. Some people had even brought food along, in case it all dragged on past lunchtime.

The meeting didn't get off to a promising start. With failing eyesight, one of the elders mistook one of the fishwives for a man! She stormed out in a dreadful huff, bawling abuse at him and anyone else who dared to laugh, including her husband. Nobody envied him going home.

The damage done to the village by the dragleon was merely an "accident" and not Nisa's fault at all, the elders quickly decided, after her parents blamed them for it, in front of everyone!

The village kitty was in great shape, after last year's bumper harvest and would pay for any repairs required and for a new village meeting house, to be built by Joseph and his crew. Everyone agreed to call it a "town hall," which the elders thought sounded very grand, while the ring of thorns would be called the "boma" from now on.

The washer woman settled down, her reputation in tact after being assured that any missing underwear would also be seen as part of the "accident" and not her fault at all, either.

The village wouldn't pay for any loss of livestock to the

leopard. No, not to snakes either.

The elders were dismayed by everyone's reaction to the driver ants. They declared that everyone must stay calm next time and that yes, alright, it had been very funny in the end. They rather lost patience however, when somebody proposed that ant costumes be made for the next Dragleon Festival. And quite how to make all the little anty legs and feelers was definitely not, they felt, a suitable topic for a village meeting, "For goodness sakes!"

So it continued, with the ins and outs and pros and cons of each and every little thing being discussed and debated, endlessly, before any decision could be reached.

Some people failed to put their hands up before speaking too, which the elders were not happy about in a public meeting.

They were not happy with the young man at the back selling beer at a public meeting, either! Although judging by the amount he sold, the rest of the village seemed only too happy about it.

After a heated debate, what to do about the missing Thabo and the problem leopard was finally agreed upon, although many of the village women weren't happy about that, having wanted to play their part. The elders were having none of it though and flatly refused to budge.

They would combine a hunt for the leopard with a loud search for Thabo, they declared. Small groups of armed men, *only*, would set out, making as much noise as possible.

While one silent hunting party would go after the leopard, having first found out from Jasmine where it was, the other groups would hopefully scare it or distract it and could also be heard by Thabo, wherever he may be. They even decided what his punishment was going to be, if it turned out that he was just being naughty again, which his parents were not happy about.

Except that one of the elders had nodded off, to loud jeers from the baying crowd. So they had to go over it, all over again, which the entire village was definitely not happy about.

As the meeting finally ended, there was a brief stampede of villagers, desperate to get out of there and get on with their sunny afternoons.

"Well, that all went better than expected, I thought," one elder said to another, pleasantly.

"Good grief, man! What were you expecting? War? Plague? Famine?"

"Oh possibly all three," he replied airily, "After debating each of them first, of course," which ended the meeting, once and for all.

The very next day at the crack of dawn, Nisa's father went to find the dragleon in her woods. He left armed with two spears and a long knife, which shocked Nisa.

"Surely you'd rather I can defend myself, if I do come across the leopard?" he reasoned.

Nisa accepted that, but gave him an extra big hug as he set off. So did her mum, she noticed.

He stopped to listen for a while at the edge of the forest, took a deep breath and entered into a world of tangled shadows. Every so often. He stopped suddenly. To listen. Nothing. So he carried on along the path until. He stopped again. Still nothing. He crept forwards, deeper into the forest.

The dragleon lay curled up on a thick carpet of African violets. It was one of her favourite glades, where he thought he might find her. As he approached he could hear her snoring gently, which stopped suddenly.

"Thought you could sneak up on me, did you?" she asked, opening one sore eye.

"Ah. Just testing, but I'll catch you out yet, one of these days. How are you feeling?"

"You won't, you know. Not here, where I've got my little spies," she told him, tapping the side of her nose, "And thank you for asking. My eyes are much better, almost as good as new."

"Good, but what do you mean; you've got your little spies?"

"My flowers sort of warn me, if you like. If I'm touching ones I've made, my scales start tingling. I don't know how it works exactly, but somehow I know what they're trying to tell me."

"What, even crops? That must be awful!"

"Oh thank goodness no! It's only the plants that pop up near me, not just anything, or something I actually sowed or planted, as such. That would drive me insane, I should think," she shuddered at the very thought of, "All those screaming crops and vegetables, getting the chop!"

"Sorry to wake you up anyway, but I thought I'd better warn you about today and tell you what went on at the village meeting," he said, raising his eyes to the heavens.

"Oh do tell. I like a bit of gossip, so don't skimp on the details, will you?"

They discussed it at some length, including the fishwife's strop, the washer woman's reputation, somebody falling asleep, somebody selling beer, the new town hall, the driver ants and the great Dragleon Festival costume debate. Jasmine was pleased to hear that people weren't blaming either her or Nisa for the damage she'd caused. She was relieved that folks seemed to be warming to the ring of thorns around the village too, the "boma." She also agreed to stay well out of the way today, but would much rather help if she could.

"You have helped. I know where to start searching now," he said and went on to explain, "If we can't kill the leopard, we want it to be scared stiff of people after today, not dragleons."

The journey back to the village was much more pleasant, with birds calling and singing throughout the forest, as if welcoming the new day, or threatening each other with blue murder!

"They'd better make the most of it," he thought to himself, "Because it's going to pour down later on, if I'm any judge. I hope everyone's up and ready, or we'll all get soaked."

Thankfully, they were. Yet it was a strange sight, to see the village so divided.

Women and children clapped and sang around the edge of the village square, while the men milled about in the centre, all of them armed with spears, long knives and bows.

Pots, pans, tins and ladles clanged and clonked together, on belts slung around their waists. They wore bracelets and anklets that rattled and gourds filled with beads tied around their necks, anything to make as much noise as possible.

Nisa's father went to tell the elders what he'd learned from Jasmine. They decided who should go with which group and spread the word. A handful of men quietly removed whatever might rattle and took off their clonking belts, handing them to their worried wives.

The men split up into their groups and headed off in different directions. Women whooped and cheered after them, egging them on to be brave, while the children followed them through the streets, but only as far as the edge of town and no further.

The men rattled their gourds and smacked their pots and pans, for all the world to hear.

She'd set off as soon as Nisa's dad had left her that morning, but even so, the distant dragleon heard them heading out of the village and into the fields and woods beyond.

The boatman led a team down to the river and upstream, but figured he'd have seen the boy from his ferry, if he'd headed out that way. They clanged and banged and called out anyway. Turtles buried deep into the mud and the crocodiles sunk beneath the surface of the river, while herons and kingfishers took flight, ahead of the oncoming noise.

Two teams headed into Jasmine's woods, but knew the leopard had not been lurking there, or the dragleon would've known about it. They rattled and clattered and yelled out anyway. Chameleons hid amongst the leaves. Foxes fled and monkeys leapt away through the tree tops. Even the distant hyenas slunk off through the bushes, with their tails between their legs.

Some followed the road that led to the crossroads and markets and villages beyond, but Thabo would've called out or stopped them, if he'd seen Nisa's parents, the day after he disappeared. They crashed and bashed and shouted out anyway. Hares skedaddled out of their way, warthogs trotted off with their tails in the air and antelope of all kinds bounded off into the bush.

The fishermen went down to the river and along towards the lake, but hadn't the dragleon been there, only the day before? Surely taking the lake road would've been quicker, yet they'd been told to avoid it. They clanked and clonked and hollered out anyway. The fish eagles beat a hasty retreat, flocks of finches fled from the reed beds and the hippos grunted and gathered in the very deepest part of the lake, watching them warily.

Nisa's dad and three others, all of whom used to be hunters, had taken the lake road.

It was the only place that Jasmine had sensed any inkling

of leopard lately, and probably guarding a kill too, so the most likely place they'd find it. Not wanting to frighten it away from their spear points and arrows, they made no sound whatsoever.

The leopard had heard enough to know that something was afoot, but he wasn't quite surrounded by the distant sounds and they weren't heading his way either. So he settled down to try and work it all out. Rather than worry, just yet.

One of the pesky jackals barked a warning to her scavenging mate, at which the leopard's ears twitched. When the snap of a twig echoed through the trees, the tip of his tail began twitching too.

Nisa's father turned sharply at the sound, to glower at the careless man who'd made it. He lowered his palms to the ground and pointed into the leaf litter, insisting on greater care. The man behind him shrugged a silent apology, before they carried on into the woods.

At the rustle of leaves, a fleeing kudu some way off, the leopard raised his head, sharply.

He sat up and snarled softly when he caught the scent of people, approaching.

While he didn't want to abandon the carcass he'd been feeding on, it was hardly worth defending by now. Little more than fly ripe scrapes of flesh on the bone. Nor could he drag it to safety up the tree. It had stubbornly stayed held fast by something, down on the forest floor. Yet if they carried on coming this way, they were sure to come across it. He doubted they'd be pleased about it either. They seemed to look after their own, these humans.

The mad noises carried on in the distance, while these few people were trying to be quiet.

All of a sudden, the leopard understood. It was a tactic he sometimes used himself, skipping after baboons in the trees

146

on the darkest of nights. Rustle a branch and leap as far away from it as possible. Wait in silence, for baboons don't see so well in the dark. Often one would scamper right into him, trying to escape from the noise it had just heard, somewhere over there. Then you had it, but he would not be had so easily. How dare they try one of his own tricks on him! He slunk down the tree head first and into some bushes nearby, to lie in wait.

The four hunters spread out among the trees, closer now. They could smell it, the leopard and the sickly sweet stench of decay. It must be resting on a kill then, probably up in a tree.

They crept closer, listening and looking up into the trees. One of them quietly took an arrow and notched it to his bow. The leopard hunkered down amongst the bushes, its lips twitching in a silent snarl. Nisa's father lowered the point of his stabbing spear, to hold it out in front of him. Those behind raised their spears to their shoulders, ready to throw, hard and fast. They came closer, unaware that the leopard was waiting for them. They kept looking up at the trees, half expecting it to rain down on them, at any moment. The bowman pulled back the string, stretching it taught and ready. The leopard flattened his ears and arched his neck, pulling his head back like a coiled spring. Step by step, the hunters inched nearer through the brush. With their eyes darting this way and that and up and down, they edged up to a small clearing. The leopard unsheathed his claws. He could see them now, through the tangle of leaves.

A cloud of flies erupted from the forest floor, like buzzing smoke that wafted upwards.

There! Nisa's father spotted the stark white of exposed bone. They moved forward to take a look, dropping their guard for a second, just as the leopard had figured they might.

That little one out in front looked like their leader, and so probably the most dangerous.

Off to one side, the bushes exploded! The leopard shot across the clearing, incredibly fast.

In a split second, Nisa's father was on his back. The leopard hurtled past him, taking out one of the hunters behind. It launched into his torso, knocking him flat. They rolled over in a flurry of leaves. It hugged him around his shoulders, pinning his arms and kicking with its hind feet.

Then it was gone. As quickly as it appeared, having taken them all by surprise.

"There was no sound," the bowman croaked, "I thought it would roar, but it didn't."

"It was just there, all of a sudden, among us," another hunter shook his head in disbelief.

"I didn't have time for a single shot. Are you alright? Oh no! You're hurt," the bowman rushed over to his friend, holding him down to stop him trying to stand.

Nisa's father sat up, his belly smarting. He managed to stand, slowly, in shock. When he lifted his hand up in front of his face, his eyes widened at the sight of glistening blood. Only then did he look down at his stomach. Four gashes where it had sliced him, just once, with one paw, as it charged right through him.

"To get away," he swallowed hard, "It was just trying to get past us. That's all."

"All! He's cut up pretty bad. Here, here and across his back, there," the bowman said.

"But it didn't bite, didn't even try. It didn't want to hang around, to fight. So it knew it was in danger. It knows the ways of man. It must've been watching us for weeks," Nisa's dad worked out. He also worked out that his was only a flesh wound, however painful it felt. He would be okay.

He and one of the huntsmen went to examine the remains

on the ground. Most of the smaller bones were missing or broken, but it was clearly a person. It had a human skull, a backbone and a pelvis, all gnawed. What were once young arms and one of the legs lay scattered, in pieces.

"But why didn't it lift him up a tree? They always take their kills up trees," Nisa's father wondered, looking around until he noticed. One of the legs had been caught in a snare. It still gripped the bare bone, holding it fast.

"It's Thabo alright," he muttered, lowering his head, "Look. What's left of his school trousers," he searched the leaf litter and knelt down, "And here's his cap, see?"

"He must've been caught in the snare, when the leopard came across him."

"Sorry. This may hurt. So brace yourself, eh?" the bowman said to the prone hunter, lifting him so he could wrap a cloth around his stomach wounds.

"AAGH!"

"I said it would hurt, didn't I? But we have to wrap it tight, to hold everything in," he winced as blossoms of red seeped through the cloth almost at once, spreading like opening flowers.

"It'll take all of us to get him back home in one piece. We'll carry him, while you keep guard. You're in no fit state to carry anything," the uninjured spearman told Nisa's dad.

"There's not enough body left to bury, is there? Poor lad. We may as well leave him here."

"But what was he doing out here? Where was he going? I mean why?" the bowman wondered.

"We'll never know for sure. He might've got away, if he hadn't been caught in a snare."

"It must've been hard for a hungry leopard, to resist such an easy kill," the spearman gulped, "Or I doubt it would've attacked at all. More often they try to steer clear of us," they all agreed.

The bowman picked up the cap and brushed it off, to take back to his parents.

They heaved and hobbled back to the village, looking like they'd been in the wars.

"Oh I've just thought. Who's going to tell his parents?" Nisa's father gulped, looking around.

"Well. Don't. Look. At. Me," the badly injured hunter managed, cracking a weak smile.

The other groups had all returned. They stood or sat around, chatting with each other and the rest of the village, eagerly awaiting any news of the leopard, or of Thabo.

As the hunting party made it through the gate, they faced a wave of bodies rushing towards them, but any hope was quickly dashed by their sorry appearance. It was all too obvious they'd come across the leopard. Yet there was no great cat to be seen, dangling limply beneath a pole, slung over their aching shoulders.

"Are you badly hurt? Was it frightened off for good d'you think? Here, let me give you a hand? Me too. Come on. Let us take the weight from now on," everyone asked, all at once.

"I'm. Not. That heavy," the injured hunter croaked.

"Did you injure it, at least? How did it get away? Was it scary? Which way did it go?" came a further barrage of desperate questions.

A woman forced her way through the press of eager bodies, breathless, silencing the crowd.

"Thabo? Did you find my boy? Where is he? Any trace of him?" his mother begged the hunting party. Her desperate eyes searched their faces, for any sign of the very news she was dreading. She found it there, in the fear behind their eyes, in the way they couldn't quite meet her gaze, in the sorry silence as their mouths opened and closed, like stranded fish.

Suddenly, her legs gave out from under her. She raised her face to the skies above and let out a jagged, heart-rending wail of grief.

The men of the village parted, as the women of the village pushed through, to get to her, to comfort her, console her, to help her to her feet.

They failed. They couldn't. There was no help to be had, at a time such as this.

There she sat and continued to sit, crumpled and crushed and wailing with grief.

Her husband joined her down on the floor, holding her, rocking her, while tears welled up in his own haunted eyes, not knowing what else to do.

"I'm so, so sorry, but there was no doubt," was all the bowman could say.

He shook his head as he handed the poor man his missing son's cap.

All the women of the village began to wail, as was the custom at such times. The sad sound spread out among them, rising and falling in a mournful rhythm that spoke of the dead, of the loss and of a mother's aching grief.

"What hopes of a funeral? The body?" one of the elders asked the hunters quietly.

"There will be no funeral. It is not possible," Nisa's dad informed him, lowering his eyes.

It began to rain. People cleared the streets, but the mournful wailing continued all around the village, from inside people's houses, from inside shops and storage sheds, from porches and from kitchen windows. While Thabo's mother sprawled in the pouring rain, being rocked gently and held up out of the mud by her heartbroken husband.

It rained and it rained, in what turned out to be the last heavy downpour of the season.

By the time the light began fade and the frogs began to call, by the time Thabo's parents had helped each other, holding each other up as they hobbled back to their home, by the time the mourning song and the rain had finally died down around the village and bats had dropped down from the eaves to flitter across the night sky; a thousand full moons filled the streets, the lanes and alleyways, reflected in their own ghostly light, in a thousand muddy puddles.

Chapter Eleven

Tomorrow was another market day, if only they could get there along the muddy track.

Nisa's parents would take Nathi to sell his fish, while Nathi's mum would watch over Nisa.

Joseph got on with clearing up the damage caused by the dragleon, while she remained in her new patch of forest. She wanted to make the most of the rains, working her magic on the trees and plants, to make it all her very own.

Everyone seemed quiet in the village that day, as they went about their business and went their separate ways. Nisa's dad was worried about his stomach wound opening up, so one of Joseph's crew went along to help, with any lifting or digging that he didn't dare do.

Her parents got both carts to the market though, without once having to dig them out.

The market was half empty of stalls, this late into the rainy season. Most of the villages round about had nothing left to sell. Only those who knew the dragleon had anything much to spare and people were beginning to notice and ask questions. How did they do it? How come their village still had food to sell? What was their secret?

They shrugged and smiled and said the secret was in their soil, or maybe the river, perhaps?

While the others did brisk business, Nisa's dad went to look for the Bushmen, but couldn't find them anywhere. They must've gone back to the desert, maybe to look for a thorn bush, to make another needle from. Or to leave their Wise One waiting, lain out all alone, as was their custom.

"Oh look Nathi. It's your little friends again," Nisa's mum

said brightly, "Now don't you go giving them too much, will you? Or your Ma will have my guts for garters. Do you hear?"

"Hello you two!" he called out, waving.

"Oh hey! It's the little Prince in his chair, with wheels on it," the boy said, smiling. They hobbled and shuffled over, looking pleased to see him, but Nathi had run right out of fish.

"I'm sorry, but I can't sell you anything today," he gestured at his empty stall, feeling terrible.

If the children were at all disappointed, they hid it very well, which earned them a free doughnut each from Nisa's mum.

They found it hard to talk whilst licking their sugary lips, so Nathi talked for all three of them, until he beckoned Nisa's mum down to whisper in her ear.

"Yes. I don't see why not. Come on then," she said, picking him up by the armpits and plonking him onto the table, "Oomph! You're getting too big for me to do that, you know?"

The children looked at them strangely, wondering what they were playing at, when Nisa's mum came round in front of the tables, armed with a damp cloth.

A worried look flashed across their faces and they shuffled backwards, out of range.

"It's alright you two. I only wanted to wipe your hands clean. They must be all sticky with the sugar and that. Come on. It's okay," she encouraged them.

"Get away! Stop pestering these people! Little beggars!" a man bellowed at them, cuffing the girl around the back of her head. She would've toppled over, but for her crutch.

"SIR! I'm dealing with these two, right now. Not you! I don't need your sort of help either and neither does she, for that matter. Unless you're buying something, kindly leave us be," Nisa's mum rounded on him with unexpected fury. She stood her ground, glowering at him.

If the children were surprised by her outburst, the man looked outraged by it. He glowered right back at her, whilst trying to think up an answer.

"I was about to ask them if they wanted a go in my chair!" Nathi broke their stalemate.

"I'd be sure to clean it afterwards then," he grumbled over his shoulder, leaving them to it.

"I had a bath, only last week!" the girl shouted after him.

"Never you mind what the likes of him say. Come on, if you'd like to?" Nisa's mum encouraged the little boy over, "I'll help you up, if you'll let me?"

His face was a picture. He wasn't used to anyone being so kind, or defending him either. Little beggar he may be, but only because he'd had to beg and for as long as he could remember. He'd even stolen things, when he was hungry enough, but somehow that didn't quite make him a thief. Not to Nathi and not to Nisa's mum. He shuffled over on his hands and his bottom, raising his arms up when he reached the chair.

"That's right. I'll lift you up under your arms, if that's okay?"

"Nah, Missus. To wipe me hands first. He was right. They're filthy. So would his be, if he had to get around like I do," he told her.

Nisa's mum tried not to laugh as she wiped them for him and lifted him up. He was so light it shocked her. She almost threw him up into the air, by accident. When she sat him in the chair, he could only just reach both the big wheels at the same time.

"You move by turning the big wheels at the back with your hands. You turn by leaning in the direction you want to go, while spinning only the other wheel," Nathi explained.

"Oh WOW! This is great!" the little boy squealed as he moved off, grinning from ear to ear, "Whoa. Thanks. Cor!

I'd love one of these. I'd roll right over his rotten foot, for starters!"

Nisa's mum walked around behind him as he got the hang of turning and stopping.

"Can I even go backwards?" he asked, "It's almost as good as having legs, I reckon!"

"Can I have a go too?" the girl asked, throwing Nathi a pleading look.

"Yes, of course," Nathi and Nisa's mum both said together, which made them smile.

The little boy with no legs quietened down as he concentrated, reversing the chair back between the tables, one of which he knocked, the first time he tried it, saying a bad word.

As Nisa's mum went to lift him up, she caught the faintest glimmer of regret, or was it sadness, behind his eyes. It almost broke her heart to see it there, but she wouldn't risk embarrassing him, by making anything of it.

The girl got into the chair with no trouble at all. She managed well enough, but wasn't quite a natural in it, like her friend. He was used to using both his arms to get about, while she wasn't and kept turning in a wide arc, when she didn't mean to. One of her arms was stronger than the other. Even so, she enjoyed it tremendously. As she got down from the chair she stared at the crutch, propped up against the stall. She wanted to kick it away and never need it again, but grabbed it roughly and stabbed it down into the dirt instead, turning around sharply.

"Thank you. That was very kind of you both. Come on," she said to her friend and was gone.

He thanked them as well, but quickly followed her, with a loyalty that touched Nisa's mum.

Nathi watched them go, with a nagging feeling that by

156

trying to brighten up their day, he'd only made their lives that bit harder to bear. He almost wished he hadn't.

Nisa was near bored to tears, doing sums set by Cecily.

She lay on her bed with her cheeks pushed up by the heels of her hands. Every so often she turned a page with a heavy sigh, feeling trapped in her room, by the boards that were back up over her window and by Cecily kneading dough in the other room, guarding the door.

A hint of movement caught the corner of her eye. She turned her head to see what it could be. Any thoughts of sums were instantly forgotten. She jumped up and leaned closer, for a better look.

Dozens of delicate lines were dropping straight down from the milk white mantis egg cases. They popped out through countless tiny holes that hadn't been there before. Each thread was as thin as cotton, but slightly thicker at one end. While she watched, one of the lines began to fray. Tiny fibres peeled back from just behind the tip. They were legs, she realised, waving about and so thin and pale you could almost see through them. The tiniest living thing she thought she'd ever seen slowly revealed itself to be a baby praying mantis, so delicate and yet so perfect.

It curled up its bottom and flexed its arms, turning its tiny head as soon as it touched something solid. More and more of the dangling threads unravelled at their tips, each of them a milk white baby mantis, being born. They flayed their fine legs, feeling around for something to cling on to, for the very first time. Some found nothing beneath them, by the time their thread had reached its full length. They dropped down into thin air, carried away on the faintest breeze of her breath. On to start a new life, to watch and wait and hunt, just as their mother had done before them.

Nisa sat still, spellbound by the tiny miracle that was taking place before her eyes, just as her father had promised. It was quite the most beautiful little thing she thought she'd ever seen.

"Don't go," she pleaded with those that wafted away, until only a few remained. They waved their front legs in the fresh air, turning their tiny white heads to look this way and that, rocking as they learned to walk, searching out a safer place to start their new lives.

She wondered where the others would go, outside in the big, wide world. Where would they choose to settle down? What would make somewhere just right, for a mantis to want to stay? What would they need or want or wish for in their lives? Plenty of juicy insects to grab hold of? Did a mantis ever wish for anything? Snakes did. That much was clear. She found herself wondering if even they could make a wish on the dragleon's magical scales, like her snake had. "What would they wish for, if they could? What would I wish for, come to think of it, if I could have another wish?" she thought about it long and hard, which was much more fun than thinking about sums. The answer, when she settled on one, surprised even her. She wondered if you could make a wish for someone else, because hers would be for Nathi's legs to work properly.

A sudden brainwave made her sit bolt upright, her mind racing.

"Of course! Why ever not? Why didn't I think of it sooner? Why can't Nathi make a wish on the dragleon's scales? Like the snake did? Like I once did?" she wondered, "Jasmine thinks the world of him, so I'm sure she'd be happy to do it and it's obvious what he'd wish for, which would be just . . . brilliant! He could walk again!"

Nisa realised that she'd babbled that last bit out loud, almost bursting with excitement.

"Who's you talking to, in there?" Cecily wanted to know.

"Oh sorry, I was just thinking out loud, about sums. I just worked a hard one out," she lied. Nisa couldn't wait to tell Nathi all about her idea, when he got back with her parents.

Nathi was quiet all the way home, with a great deal on his mind. He realised how lucky he was, compared to some. Thanks to his chair, he could do most anything he wanted, while those poor children couldn't. There was one thing he couldn't do though, or so he'd always been told. He couldn't help feeling that maybe he should try, simply because, they couldn't. It felt like he was wasting his own good fortune, when they had none, which didn't seem fair somehow. It wasn't right. Nathi swallowed hard, deciding there and then, that he should go and play in the woods.

It wasn't allowed at the moment though, because of the leopard, stalking the village. But hadn't they scared it off, only yesterday? Everyone said so. It must be miles away by now and he could always arm himself, he supposed. That way, even if he did come across it, he might end up a hero! Now that would give *would* give them something to think about, in school.

Nisa's mum and dad got back in the early afternoon, dropping Nathi off to make his own way home through the village, as usual. They drove the donkeys up to their shed and walked home.

Having thanked Cecily, who thanked them in return, they sat down and listened to Nisa babbling on excitedly about the mantis egg cases hatching.

Only she was so excited that she went on to blurt out the brilliant idea she'd had, about Nathi making a wish on Jasmine's scales, like she once did. Wouldn't it be wonderful!

Her parents looked to each other, speechless. Smiles crept across their faces as it dawned on them. It would indeed be wonderful, wouldn't it? He could walk again, couldn't he?

They told Nisa to wait a moment, while they discussed it in the next room. She sat on the edge of her bed for what seemed like ages, jiggling. At least they were taking her seriously. So they must believe her now, for certain. It felt like a great weight had been lifted off her shoulders.

"Who knew secrets could feel so heavy?" she said out loud, to see if she still could, properly.

It sounded okay. Nisa breathed a sigh of relief because she was still talking clearly.

Her parents reached a decision and braced themselves, knowing that she wasn't going to like it. This wish idea was too big and important for her to blurt it out to Nathi, just like that. He didn't know about the dragleon being able to grant wishes, did he? Nor did Joseph or Cecily and they'd have to convince them that it was even possible first, which wasn't going to be easy. They promised not to mention what Nisa had wished for, in case it spoiled it, but forbid her from going to see or talk to Nathi at all, before they'd had a chance to talk to both his parents first.

"But it was my idea! It's not yours to tell, or his mum and

dad's either! Why do grown-ups always have to spoil things?" she scowled, sticking her chin out and folding her arms.

"Because sometimes we know better than you what's best for our children," her dad insisted.

Nisa could tell there'd be no arguing with him. His jaw jutted out and he folded his arms when he wasn't about to budge. She looked down and quickly unfolded her own arms.

"We'll ask if you can be the one to actually tell him about it. It was your idea after all," her mum tried to soften her up, "You can be the one who asks Jasmine too, if you like?" she tried.

She would like, but it wouldn't be the same. They'd spoiled it. Nisa frowned at them both.

She was left on her own and sworn to stay in her room, while her parents went to see Cecily.

Nathi wasn't home yet, which neither surprised nor concerned her in the slightest.

"He's most likely gone to his little shed. Sorry, his 'workshop,' he calls it now. Just like his dad's," Cecily explained with a smile. Joseph wasn't there either, still out at work.

"Just what are you two grinning about anyway? I can tell you're up to something daft, but what can be so important, that I has to go get him from work, eh?" she eyed them suspiciously.

"Trust us, it'll be worth it. Just you wait and see," Nisa's mum grinned. They both did. They couldn't help it. They could hardly wait to see the look on both their faces.

Cecily bustled off, shaking her head and tutting away to herself.

They waited a long time for her to return, with a rather grumpy Joseph, who'd been busy.

Chapter Twelve

Nathi had indeed gone to his workshop, but only briefly to pick up his parrot, a knife and a sharp stick. After that, he trundled out through the river gate as bold as brass and turned off across the clearing. It was a rough path and his parrot bobbed up and down a bit on the back of his chair, but he'd wheeled across it many times before, always stopping at the edge of the forest.

This time he didn't stop though. He carried on as leaves and branches loomed overhead, into a world of dappled shade, with strange plants and noises. Just birds mostly, or insects, he knew.

He wouldn't go far. He hoped he wouldn't have to, because Jasmine was sure to find him. Nisa said she always found her, sooner or later.

"And she'll be well on her way back by now," he said to himself, as much as his parrot.

Nathi forced the wheels of his chair round along the bumpy path, up over exposed tree roots and sploshing through shallow puddles that dotted the track, deeper into the darker forest.

His parrot gripped the back of the chair as if its life depended on it, bobbing and weaving to hold on. Once or twice it let out a squawk, when the chair came down with a bit of a bump.

"I'm doing it though, aren't I? I'm here, playing in the forest, sort of. I knew I could do it! So this is what it's like, eh?" he said to himself and his parrot, stopping to reach around and tickle him under his chin. The bird stretched out its neck and half closed its eyes in bliss.

Nathi stood his stick upright in the soil, as if planting a flag. He sat still, just to look around and take it all in, to listen and really hear things, for once.

A lizard scampered up a tree trunk, following a twisting vine. A bullfrog squatted beside the path, guarding a puddle, full of tadpoles. There were more butterflies around than he'd ever seen, fluttering about in the still forest air. A pied crow cawed at him from high up in the trees. A pair of pretty finches darted off through the leaves, twittering away to each other. His parrot squawked back at the crow, as if answering some insult, with one of its own.

"Sorry if I've left you behind a bit lately, but you won't come fishing with me and I can't take you to school or the markets. Not with your big mouth, now can I?" Nathi explained.

Everything around him was green and growing and dotted with different coloured flowers. Bees buzzed by, from one to another. Lizards scuttled after beetles through the leaves on the forest floor. Crickets chirped, unseen. Birds called up above, hidden among the tangle of leafy branches.

"It's beautiful and I never even knew," Nathi sighed to himself.

He heard a snort from somewhere off to his left and another, not far off through the trees.

"It's only impala, calling in alarm. They won't hurt you," he told his parrot when it flinched.

The first of the herd came prancing through the bush, jumping the path as if it were a stream.

Another bounded by, right in front of him and yet more behind, gracefully leaping through the air and jinking as they landed with startling ease. Nathi watched, spellbound. A couple more sailed past, clearing the track in breath-taking bounds and swiftly leaping off again. The ram with his lyre-shaped horns, was the last to run by, still snorting in alarm, urging the others on and away.

"See? Beautiful," Nathi said to his parrot and sighed to himself.

"I wonder what spooked them like that though," he said out loud, gripping his wheels to move on, "Probably just us, come to *think* of it," Nathi grunted, with unexpected effort.

Looking down, he saw that one of his front wheels had wedged between two roots. He tried to pull the chair backwards. It spun round a little, but the wheel held fast.

He tried to push forwards again, but still the wheel stayed snagged.

With one almighty shove, he pushed down *really hard*, to go *forwards*.

With a soft "crack!" the wheel snapped off. The chair lurched forwards, toppling over.

Nathi landed with a grunt, sprawled on the dirt track and gasping for breath, winded by the weight of the chair on top of him. He struggled to haul himself out from under it, clawing at the mud and gasping for breath. He struggled again and again, but got nowhere.

Stopping to try and catch his breath, he noticed the bullfrog had not budged.

He tried again, straining and heaving harder still, gouging grooves into the soft earth with his fingers, but still stuck fast. There was nothing solid to hold onto, only leaves and mud.

His parrot walked up to him, comical, rocking, peering at his face with its head on one side.

The squat bullfrog shifted its position slightly, the better to face both threats.

Nathi began to wonder what he was going to do, trapped by his own stupid chair.

He tried to push up, rather than pull forwards, shouting out of pure frustration, as if yelling might give him the strength he needed! It didn't. He relaxed his arms, slumping, defeated.

At the risk of horrible embarrassment, Nathi realised that he needed help. The thought of having to explain himself made him feel quite sick, but there was nothing else for it.

"Help!" he called out, weakly at first, but knew it wouldn't be enough, "HELP!" he shouted, louder this time, "That's better," he thought, getting used to the idea.

"HELP! Someone PLEASE HELP!" he yelled even louder.

The bullfrog puffed itself up at him, raising up on its bowed, bandy legs.

He carried on calling out, until he realised he was wasting his breath. There was nobody around to hear him. Except for a fat frog, which was gaping at him now, hissing.

"Oh Nisa, I wish you'd come with me. I know you'd help. NISA!" he called.

"NISA! NISA!" the parrot squawked, tilting his head as if working something out. He started bobbing up and down on the spot and all of a sudden, flew off!

The bullfrog settled back down, into its flabby squat once more.

"Hey you, come back here! Don't leave me, you stupid bird!" Nathi shouted after it, "Well charming! Thanks a bunch," he grumbled.

The parrot disappeared through the trees, still squawking.

Nisa had waited long enough, she thought she might just sneak out and find Nathi, before the grown-ups got to him first. She had a good idea where he'd be, if he hadn't gone home already. If he had, she could slink back inside and her parents would be none the wiser. She crept out of the front door and headed for his workshop, as he liked to call it. No sooner had she got there, than his blessed parrot turned up, flapping madly on a perch, right in front of her face.

"Nisa! NISA!" it squawked its head off, still flapping madly, threatening to give her away.

"SSSHH! Shut up, you stupid bird!" she hissed and went to cover its mouth with her hands, but quickly stopped herself. You couldn't really cover a beak, especially one that might bite.

"Nisa! NISA!" the parrot screeched, again and again, "Nisa! NISA!" over and over again.

"Shut up, I said! You'll get me into trouble," she snarled at it.

The parrot fluttered off and squawked her name again. It flew back to her, still calling. It flew off again, screeching at her, landing, turning around and bobbing up and down.

Even for him, it was strange behaviour, acting like he was desperate about something.

The parrot fluttered back to her. It simply would not let up.

"Nisa! NATHI! Nisa! NATHI!" it tried, almost beside itself, "NATHI! NATHI!"

"What are you . . . ? What do you mean? Is something wrong . . . with Nathi? Where is he?" the penny finally dropped, "Is he hurt somewhere? Can you take me to him? Go on. Show me!"

The parrot flew off, screeching Nathi's name, only this time, Nisa followed. He landed, turned and squawked both their names. As he flew off again, Nisa broke into a run.

The leopard had been stalking a herd of impala, when something had spooked them. He doubted it was him, but they'd bounded off through the bush. He began to follow the fleeing herd, unhurried. Sooner or later he'd manage to sneak up on them, unnoticed and close enough to strike.

When he heard a human calling he stopped, dead in his tracks. It unnerved him. He didn't want anything to do with humans, not after the day before. They were more trouble than they were worth. The shouting stopped and a parrot screeched, strangely. The sound grated on his nerves as it flew off through the forest, still squawking. He grew curious about the strange goings-on and edged closer, for a better look.

Nisa ran across the village clearing. Something bad had happened to Nathi, but she didn't dare call him yet, afraid of being discovered. Only once she reached the trees, running after his parrot, running out of breath, did she risk yelling out to him.

The leopard edged around in a wide and wary arc, circling the spot where he'd heard the human calling. With each and every careful step, he tested the leaves with the outside edge of a paw to see if they'd rustle, before putting his foot down. Creeping closer and closer, until he could see what all the fuss was about, unseen himself.

He watched through a veil of leaves and he remembered. It was that injured boy, sprawled on the path; helpless, plump and alone. Trapped by the chair on top of him, it looked like and oh, that last one had tasted so good. Better than dog, even. The leopard licked his lips.

The bullfrog had gone, Nathi noticed, leaving his precious puddle unguarded.

The parrot flew ahead of Nisa, screeching still, down a track that she knew well.

"Into the woods? What's he playing at? Are you sure?" she called after the bird.

"NATHI! I'm coming! NATHI! Can you hear me?" she shouted, still racing after his parrot.

The leopard heard her. His head snapped up, rustling the leaves.

Nathi heard it, turned his head and saw him, sitting there. He SCREAMED!

"I'm COMING! Hold ON!" Nisa heard him and called

ahead.

She ran as fast as she could, catching up with his parrot, racing along the path, shouting out.

The leopard thought better of it and slunk off, snarling bitterly over his shoulder.

Nisa rounded a bend and charged up to Nathi. She heaved the heavy chair off him and helped him to sit up, lifting him under his arms.

"I've wet myself," he whined, twisting around to look up at her.

As his face began to quiver, Nisa squatted down on the dirt track next to him.

"It's alright. It's okay. I'm here now. It's all over."

If only it was.

"But, how did you know?" Nathi sniffled, while she had to think about it for a second.

"It was your parrot! He told me. He came to me for help," she said, amazed, but he had. There was no doubt about it, "So maybe he's not such a stupid bird, after all?"

"I keep telling people that, but they never believe me, until now."

Nathi's eyes suddenly widened, as something horrific dawned on him.

"The leopard! Where's the leopard? It was here. Right there!" he gasped, looking past Nisa.

A low gggggggrowl rumbled out of the bushes, as if to answer him.

It was still there, watching both of them now.

Chapter Thirteen

Nisa jumped up and grabbed the wheelchair, wrestling it around to face the chilling sound. Nathi scrabbled in the dirt for his sharp stick and held it out in front of him, point first like a trembling, spindly spear.

The leaves rustled and parted as the leopard's face pushed through. It snarled slowly, deeply, stepping forth and staring at the children. With stone cold eyes they would never forget.

"Thabo must've seen those same eyes," Nisa thought, with a shiver that danced down her spine. She rattled the chair desperately. Nathi brandished his stick, while the leopard oozed out from the bushes, never taking those eyes off them.

He began to circle the children. His tail flicked up and down with a flash of white, padding sideways on to them, up and down with a flicker of white. He arched his neck, head down, ready to spring at any moment. Round and round and still fluttering the tip of that tail, up and down and snow white, just beneath the tip, hoping to distract them with it for that one, split second.

Nathi shuffled around on one hand, still holding the stick out in front of him, staring at that flickering tail. He couldn't take his eyes off it. His fingers found and closed around the knife.

Nisa rattled the chair around, trying to keep it between them, mindful of Nathi's legs. It wasn't easy, meeting the leopard's gaze and refusing to watch that flirting tail, not daring shift her gaze for a moment. She knew it would launch an attack if she did. "Like lightening," her dad had said.

The leopard's ears flattened. He stopped circling, to raise a paw instead.

The children braced themselves. Nisa picked up the broken wheel. Nathi raised the knife.

It spat and tensed, surging forwards, slapping the ground, quick as a flash, testing them.

Nisa raised the wheel, threatening to throw it. Nathi closed his eyes and dropped the knife. He recovered quickly, picking it up, but the leopard had learned all it needed to know, for this.

She had nothing, not really, while he was too frightened to put up a fight. This should be easy, the leopard decided, even as the ground began to tremble beneath their feet. They all felt it, rumbling like a distant earthquake, but Nisa had felt it before.

"Jasmine?" she whispered, looking up.

The leopard attacked, instantly, lunging in low.

Nathi flinched and yelped, while Nisa squeaked and hurled the wheel. It hit the leopard's nose, stopping the cat in its tracks for that one, split second.

Having heard Nathi's cries for help, the dragleon hurtled through the forest like a runaway train. She hadn't stopped to think, charging blindly down the path. She almost ploughed right through them. It was all she could do to stop!

The children screamed, ducking behind the chair, as the leopard leapt past them.

Jasmine skidded to a halt in a spray of leaves. Lunging, she grabbed hold of its tail and pulled the leopard back. It spat and scratched and kicked at her arm, useless against her thorny scales. It curled around and tried to bite, but her free hand grasped the scruff of its neck. She wrestled with the struggling leopard, stretching it out and pinning it to the ground.

The children didn't dare to look, cowering where they hid.

The dragleon breathed in sharply, closed her eyes and

thought of sleep. She breathed out, long and hard, while the leopard spat in her face. It soon stopped struggling so viciously and finally, gave up snarling altogether. The leopard slumped into a deep, deep sleep, snoring softly instead, to bother them no more.

The children risked peeping up over the chair, as Jasmine let go of the leopard at last. Her thorny skin shrank back into softer, flower petal scales.

Nisa jumped up for a hug. Jasmine rocked her from side to side for a while, set her down gently and stepped over to Nathi.

"Hey little man, how are you?" she asked softly, "And just what have you been playing at?"

Nathi hung his head, mumbling that he'd only been trying to play in her woods.

"Like I always wanted to, but I've only gone and wet myself," he sniffled.

Jasmine figured he felt bad enough already, without her making him feel any worse.

"Don't you worry about wetting yourself, after fighting off a leopard! You were very brave, both of you, but we're going to have to tell your parents all about it, you know?"

Nisa gasped and slapped a hand to her forehead.

"Oh no. Of course! We're in BIG trouble! My parents don't know I'm here, any more than yours do. I'm supposed to stay in my room and not talk to you, not until they've told your parents about it first! There's no way we can get out of this one. That's what they're doing right now Nathi, waiting for you! Or fetching me, so I can tell you myself! We've had it!" she groaned.

"Tell me about what myself? No – yourself?" asked Nathi, wondering what she was on about.

"About making a wish on Jasmine's scales, like I did! Oh

171

I'm sorry. I shouldn't have said anything, or asked you in front of him. Sorry, but I'm all muddled up now and I don't know what to do for the best," she looked to Jasmine and back at Nathi, desperately.

"Right. Hold on. It's okay Nisa. You couldn't help it and I'll tell them so. Now let's just get this mess sorted out, shall we?" the dragleon pinched the bridge of her snout, trying to think things through. Everything seemed to be happening all at once, as it so often did around Nisa.

"Could I? Wish for something, I mean," asked Nathi, scarcely able to believe it.

"Yes, you can, I promise, but all in good time. First Nisa, you're going to have to fetch all four of your parents. Tell them what's happened. Tell them anything you like, but I need them here and I need them to bring me a dog, a goat and Donkey. Oh and a chicken too. Why not?"

"Why me? They're going to kill me," Nisa fretted.

"I don't care how you do it, but do it you must and I don't care if they tell you off. I can't leave the leopard alone like this, or Nathi alone with it. So it has to be you who goes, I'm afraid."

"But Mum and Dad will want me to wish for what they want! I know they will!"

"They won't, Nathi. It won't work like that. Trust me," Jasmine assured him and winked, "Well? What're you waiting for?" she clapped her hands at Nisa, to hurry her along.

Nisa ran off and left the two of them alone, if that's possible.

Jasmine took a deep breath, just so she could breathe out again, slowly.

"And calm down. Everything will be okay. It's okay already," she smiled and so sweetly that everything did feel okay, already. Nathi smiled back weakly, looking up at her.

"As I walk along, and you know I never drop you, try to

think really hard about what you'd most like, or what you'd most like to be able to do, perhaps. Take off your shoes first though."

"Are we doing it now? My wish? Before they even get here? Is that why you winked? Is that what you meant? Are we?" he asked, jiggling up and down and already pulling his shoes off.

"Yes, we are," Jasmine nodded, "Try to think about what you'd like to eat whilst you're at it and keep your hands flat on my scales. That's all there is to it. Okay Nathi . . . Wish away!"

The dragleon carried him beside the path, dragging his bare feet through the leaf litter. Her flower petal scales began to pulse with pale, pastel colours, which grew deeper and richer and pulsed more quickly, while Nathi made his magical wish.

All the colours of the rainbow and more besides flashed before his wide open eyes. He felt a warmth deep down inside, as his heart of hearts gave up its deepest secrets, gladly. His bare feet dragged through the dirt while Jasmine's scales throbbed away, with every colour he'd ever seen. Two of her scales shed like miracles, slipping out and wafting like flower petals on the gentlest of breezes, to land softly on the forest floor. Where they landed her scales sprouted leaves that opened up, revealing delicate curling shoots. The green shoots flowered and swelled at their tips, while Nathi watched in wonder. They fattened, ballooning yellow, round, rich and ripe.

"Oh you like melons, eh?" Jasmine lifted him up. He wrapped his arms around her neck and hugged her, burying his face in her soft scales, which slowly ceased their rainbow thrumming.

"Thank you," he whispered in her ear and kissed her gently on the cheek.

A single sunflower popped up beside her, blooming bright

yellow against the forest gloom.

"Now all you need to do is eat them, and wait for your wish to come true," she told him, leaning forwards so he could reach down and pick the first of the melons.

It was so ripe, it opened up easily. He slurped the sweet, watery flesh from its thick skin.

"Do I eat the skin and the pips and everything?" he asked, pulling a face.

"Not if you don't want to," she chuckled, "And I can hear the others coming, but they're a way off yet. So you've got time to eat the second one, if you want to?"

He did too, guzzling the melon's soft flesh and slurping up its sweet juice. His hands got all sticky and wet. Juice dribbled down his chin, which made him giggle.

"Whatever happens, no matter how much they ask, you mustn't tell anyone what you wished for. Not even Nisa or me. Do you understand?"

"I won't, I promise. Does that stop it working, your wish?" he asked her.

"It might. I don't know, but do you want to take that risk?"

He shook his head and burped! His breath smelt all melony, which had them both laughing.

They were still laughing when his parents rushed up, dragging a dog and a goat. They were closely followed by Nisa and her parents, with Donkey and a chicken, dangling by its feet.

"Oh. Have you done it already? You could've waited for us," Joseph reached up for Nathi, who fell into his father's waiting arms.

"I did it. We did a wish and it was amazing. Wow! So many colours, Dad. It was magic!"

Cecily clasped her hands to her chest, almost in tears. She and Joseph hugged their son between them, making a Nathi sandwich.

"Put him down to see if he can walk. Mind, it'll take him a while to get used to his legs working, I should think," Cecily could hardly wait.

Donkey walked up to the dragleon, wanting a good scratch behind his ears. He caught sight of the leopard and turned away, but Jasmine managed to catch his halter and breathed in his face, calming him down. The air smelt of fresh flowers, suddenly.

The dog began snarling and the goat began to struggle, having noticed the sleeping leopard.

The dragleon took hold of their leads, which they weren't happy about either, until she breathed her sweet scented breath on them too, which calmed them down as well.

The chicken seemed perfectly calm already, dangling limply from Nisa's dad's hand.

"You might not want to put him down just yet, given what I have in mind," Jasmine warned Joseph, taking hold of the chicken as well. "Thank you," she remembered to say.

Donkey followed on his own, but the chicken began to flap. So she breathed on it quickly, walking the animals over to the leopard and settling them down, right next to it.

"This can't really wait, I'm afraid," Jasmine explained, before sucking in great gulps of air. The whole of her chest swelled up, so this was going to be big, Nisa guessed.

"She's not going to wake that thing up, is she? What about the children? Nisa, come here!"

"It's alright, Daddy. You'll see. Trust her," Nisa knelt down next to Donkey, draping her arm over his shoulder as Jasmine breathed right out again. Long and slow and above all . . . calm.

The scent of flowers was almost overwhelming, strangely peaceful and softening to the senses.

175

"Well, this is nice, isn't it?" the dragleon said brightly, "All good friends together, eh?"

The leopard blinked and opened his eyes, no longer staring fiercely, but kindly and calm instead. He raised his head as Donkey stood up, leaning forward to nuzzle him. He rubbed his cheek along Donkey's nose and stood up himself, groggily at first, but soon finding his feet.

He writhed playfully around Donkey's legs and rubbed his cheek along the goat's side. His tail weaved and wafted in Jasmine's face. When the dog jumped up to lick his chin, the leopard held her down with one paw, settling down to wash her face, like his mother had when he was a cub.

"It's a miracle!" Nisa's dad gasped, but braced himself when the leopard turned to Nisa.

She held out her little hands to cup his face and scratch his cheeks. It looked like he was smiling! The leopard writhed around her, nearly knocking her over with his flanks.

He flopped over onto his back, with all four paws in the air, so she could tickle his tummy. He writhed around in bliss, batting her arms gently with great, soft paws.

The chicken toddled over and stepped up onto him, clearly feeling left out. It sat on his chest, rocking to keep its balance and clucking contentedly.

Donkey, the dog and the goat surrounded the lolling leopard, nuzzling him as he took it in turns to rub his cheeks along their faces, one after the other. It seemed incredible! It was incredible!

"Can I have a go?" begged Nathi, struggling to join in.

"It needs a grown-up over here too," Jasmine looked to Joseph, who gulped, but stepped forward. He sat Nathi down so he could stroke the leopard, scarcely believing what he was doing.

Nathi was delighted. The leopard decided that he deserved

a cheek-rubbing too, followed by Joseph himself. He was stroking a leopard, actually stroking it! And it seemed to be loving every minute of it, like a big soppy puppy, happily greeting its owner.

The others came over and all had a go, smiling at each other like children, full of wonder.

The leopard got up and wafted his tail around them, rubbing his flanks along their legs and lifting his chin so they could tickle it, rubbing his cheeks on man and beast alike.

After a while he headed off, into the forest for a drink. He looked back only once, blinking slowly at all of them, which was his way of saying goodbye, to his new best friends, forever.

Everyone sighed to see him go, even Nisa's dad, who he'd injured only the day before.

"He won't bother anyone any more. He won't chase after chickens, donkeys, goats or dogs again either, unless he wants a cuddle of course," Jasmine smiled after him, happy with her work, "And he won't be leaving the area any time soon, allowing another leopard to move on in. So you can all sleep safe and sound in your beds and for a good few years yet," she finished, with a sigh.

They still couldn't quite believe it. They'd just been fussing a leopard, and a man-eating leopard, at that! Poor Thabo, they remembered.

"Jasmine, you're a genius. Much better than our way of dealing with it, which failed miserably," Nisa's dad admitted, raising a careful hand to the bandages round his stomach.

"Couldn't have done it if Nathi hadn't been so stupid," she turned to glower at him, winking.

"But why can't he walk yet?" Cecily regained her wits first and began to worry, "You said he could, if he made a wish on Jasmine, but look at him, still sitting there like that!"

"Maybe it didn't work. It can't have. Something went wrong. I don't know," Joseph scratched his head, "Try to stand up, Nathi. Go on. Try, for me and your mum," he encouraged him.

Nathi tried, but couldn't stand up.

"Come on Nathi. Get up! You can do it now. You just wished for it, didn't you? You must have!" Nisa's mum joined in, but his legs simply would not work.

"Come on. You can do it if you try, surely?" Cecily began to sound desperate, backing away from him with a hand over her mouth.

Nathi tried again, pushing up with his arms, but it was no use. His legs refused to work. He looked to his parents, terrified of the growing disappointment on their faces.

Nisa squatted down next to him, glowering at the grown-ups.

"Come on. Stand up, for once in your life! It's *easy*. Just do it!" his dad began to sound angry.

"He CAN'T! Can't you see that? Just leave him alone! All of you!" Nisa snapped.

"Nisa! I know you're upset, but that's no excuse to talk to a grown-up like that. Any grown-up, but especially not me! Or our friends!" she added, "How dare you?"

"But Mummy, can't you see? You're upsetting him, all of you. It's not his fault, if his wish wasn't what we thought it would be," Nisa defended him, "The dummy!" sort of.

"Please everyone, let's calm down. Let Nathi speak for himself," Nisa's dad suggested.

"Okay, son, what *did* you wish for? Surely it was just to walk?" Joseph asked, shrugging.

"I can't tell you that though, or it might not come true," Nathi dared to object.

"Don't you want to be normal and walk like everyone else?"

178

Cecily demanded, unhelpfully.

"But I'm quite happy in my chair, Mum. I can't remember what it's like to walk. So how could I wish for it? Why would I anyway, when I'm happy as I am?" Nathi tried to explain.

"Well that's about the *stupidest* thing I ever heard! Even from you, boy!" Joseph blustered, turning away and pinching the bridge of his nose, "GOOD GRIEF, child!" he shouted.

"I'M SORRY IF I'M NOT HOW YOU WANT ME TO BE!" Nathi closed his eyes and shouted back, "Not really. When I thought I was, all this time, because you told me not to complain about being in my chair, not ever! You and Mum together, taught me not to mind and now I don't mind. Really I don't. Yes, sometimes it's a pain, like today, but other people fall over and break their legs or tread on thorns and that's a pain for them, except that my legs never hurt."

His voice had softened, while he tried in vain to explain.

"Look. Your mother and I just want what's best for you. We want you to be happy. That's all."

"But that's what I'm trying to *tell* you! I already am!" Nathi insisted, "Whether I can walk, or not. There's children far worse off than me. I've seen them, I've met them and they're nice."

"You mean those little cripples at that market? I knew we should never have taken him!"

"Whoa. Hang on there, Cecily. Maybe he's got a point? You brought him up to be happy with his lot and now you're telling him and us that he shouldn't have been, all along. Even I'm confused, but I think I get what he's trying to say and I'm sorry Nathi," Nisa's mum declared.

"What're you apologising to *him* for, for goodness *sakes*?" Joseph snapped at her.

Nisa's dad opened his mouth to stand up for his wife, but didn't get the chance.

"For making him feel like he's not really good enough and never really was, after all. For NOT thinking he's good enough and even *telling* him as much! I did, we all did, just now! What was I *thinking* of? When of course he's good enough. Better than good enough. Just as you are," Nisa's mum smiled down at him.

"Why can't you just be happy, that I'm happy as I am?" Nathi pleaded with his parents and turned to the only one there who'd said nothing so far, for her help.

"Look! There must be something that means more to Nathi than walking again. It's his wish and for whatever his heart desires, deep down, which even his thoughts can't change, never mind yours, when all's said and done. And it is done now, so getting upset about it won't do any good. It won't change anything. It can't. It will only upset Nathi and I think he's had enough upset for one day, don't you?" Jasmine declared, which shut everyone up. She yawned widely.

"Okay! It's our fault. I get it," Joseph raised his eyes, "We did too good a job on him, so he's just blown the ONE CHANCE he EVER had of walking again!"

"I think the dummy's actually trying to thank you for it," Nisa suggested.

"Yes, I am. By helping me and teaching me not to mind, deep down where it matters, both of you, all of you," he looked from his parents to Nisa and Jasmine, "have made way for my real wish to come true, I hope," Nathi hung his head, hoping they'd understand at last.

"Okay. So be it. I guess we gave it a try, at least," Cecily gave in, shaking her head.

"No. You succeeded, whatever his wish turns out to be," Jasmine corrected her kindly.

Cecily nodded tearfully, disappointed still, even as she reached down for Nathi's hand.

Poor Jasmine yawned again, so very tired after using so much of her magic. She said her farewells and headed off to her favourite glade, smothered in a comfy cushion of African violets. It wasn't far off, which was just as well, unless she was planning on sleep-walking there.

They sat Nathi on Donkey on the way back to the village. He enjoyed the ride, while his dad dragged the broken chair along behind him. It would be easy enough to fix.

"We might not know what he wished for, but at least we know that we did a good job. He's happy, despite everything. He must be. Kids, eh?" Joseph said to his wife, shaking his head.

"I suppose it'll all come out in the wash, unlike his shorts. We'll have to buy him a new pair now," Cecily sounded like she'd given up, "Never a dull moment, eh?"

"Not with our two, that's for sure," Nisa's mum could only agree with her on that one.

"I am here. I can hear you and I can pay for my own new shorts, too," Nathi pointed out.

As soon as he got the chance, he reached down to flick the back of Nisa's ear. Hard!

"OW! You!"

"Call me a dummy, would you?" he got her back, grinning again already.

Chapter Fourteen

A week went by, a week of unbroken sunshine, of boring school and more fishing after school. Yet still, Nathi couldn't walk. His parents did their best to hide their disappointment, but couldn't help wondering what he'd wished for instead. Even Nisa was curious, but knew better than to ask because he couldn't tell her anyway.

There didn't seem to be any change to Nathi at all, except in class sometimes. He kept shocking everyone and especially his teacher. Whenever he put his hand up or opened his mouth to speak, all eyes now turned to him, waiting to see what on earth he'd come out with next.

Gloria knocked on their door to ask Joseph and Cecily if she might have a quiet word.

"Um, has Nathi been reading any new books lately? Or made friends with a doctor, perhaps?"

"No. He doesn't have any books. Hasn't mentioned meeting anyone new, has he?"

Cecily shook her head, "But why?" She answered Gloria, with a question of her own.

"Well, I'm sure I don't understand it then," his teacher seemed mystified.

"Understand what, Gloria? He's usually quite good in class, isn't he?" Cecily frowned.

"Oh yes, very good. Only, well, *recently* . . . I'm afraid I don't know quite how to put this."

"Put *what*, Gloria? What's going on, *recently*?" Joseph was growing impatient.

"Um, when it comes to anything, anything at all you understand, of a *medical* nature, how the body works, that sort of thing. Um, young Nathi knows better than I do, all of a sudden. Better than anyone probably, in fact. It would appear he's become something of a medical genius, overnight as it were," she said, looking helpless, "I was wondering. Did you know?"

His parents looked at each other, speechless, while something seemed to dawn on them both.

"No, but that's splendid isn't it? Let's not knock it, eh Gloria," Joseph recovered first.

"No. I'll ask him if he's decided to be a doctor, shall I? That would explain it, wouldn't it?"

"Well no, not really because you see, I do wonder where all this sudden knowledge has come from. It really is quite something, I assure you and I mean, well, how? He's only a little boy."

"Ah, but a very special little boy. Once he gets an idea into his head, he's away."

"Yes. Always was on the quiet. Perhaps he's just less shy nowadays. That can't be a bad thing, now can it?" Cecily smiled, "But thanks for letting us know, how he's coming out of his shell."

"Good of you to take the time, Gloria, when I'm sure you'll be wanting to get home and put your feet up, after a hard day's teaching, eh?" Joseph hinted, clearly wanting to close the door.

"Um, yes, no. Not at all, I'm sure," Gloria finished, without feeling at all satisfied. Instead she left with a sneaky feeling that they both knew something which she didn't.

The following day was a market day and half the village had set off early.

Nisa was miffed about not being allowed to go, until it dawned on her that she could spend the day with Jasmine and out in their woods again, since the soppy leopard was no longer a threat.

She had to wait a long time for her because Jasmine never was an early riser, given the choice.

It was a different, much bigger market to their usual one.

Nathi had insisted on going, because he wanted to spend some money at last. He reckoned there'd be more of the stuff he needed at the bigger market, whatever stuff that was.

The boatman did a roaring trade that morning, since this market lay on the other side of the river. His was the only boat that could carry passengers and everyone needed to cross, for a small fee. People had to queue up and wait for the next crossing, or the next. They'd all need to cross back again later as well, for another small fee, which he was really looking forward to.

"They all add up, your small fees," he said to Nathi, rubbing his hands together gleefully.

When they got there, the market was already bustling with people from miles around. The range of goods seemed incredible to Nathi, some of it laid out on tables, some on wooden stalls with a roof, for shade. Some of it simply spread out on mats or blankets on the floor and some in cages, or makeshift pens made of wicker hurdles, which were mostly animals, but all manner of interesting bits and bobs made of metal or wood, with some bigger items in amongst.

As soon as he'd had a look round, Nathi returned to his stall, keen to sell as much as he could, as quickly as possible. He and Nisa's mum worked well together again, passing customers on to each other, with a smile and a secret wink. Cecily helped them both out and Joseph too, once he'd bought what he needed to start work on the new town hall, as the elders were already calling it.

Nathi made a small fortune for such a young man. Everyone from their village did though, which confused people from all the other villages. Just how had they managed such a bumper harvest last year and where were all these fish and beautiful cut flowers coming from?

It was the market's main topic of gossip, along with the general lack of rain this year.

Anyone from villages up in the hills didn't agree though. They'd had a terrible time of it, with more rain than even their elders could remember. Some had even been flooded out, the big lake up there having risen right over the tops of their houses. They'd had to seek shelter in the caves, up among the cliffs. Whilst everyone felt sorry for them, they were more concerned with next year's crops and how they'd fare in such parched fields.

Their tales of woe solved one mystery though. The big lake being so full would explain why the river was running so high, despite the lack of rain.

As soon as he'd sold his last fish, Nathi was off! Since Nisa's mum was all but done, she left Cecily to sell whatever was left on her stall and joined Nathi on his shopping spree. He wanted to buy too much to carry back and forth to their stalls. So she was needed to take Donkey and the cart around the market, following on behind him. Nisa's mum drove it carefully, while Joseph led Donkey by his halter, asking people to mind their backs. He stood behind his son whatever he bought, making sure that nobody diddled him. If anything, people gave him a very good price on most of the strange bits and bobs he wanted. Although why he could possibly want most of it, or what he planned on doing with it, was beyond Joseph.

"Why can't I have a son who just wants to buy toys, eh?" he joked with Nisa's mum, whilst loading a metal chair up onto the cart.

"I do want to buy a toy. Now where was that man selling wood carvings?" Nathi wondered.

His last purchase was a small wooden giraffe, beautifully carved, for Nisa.

"What on earth is all that junk for?" Cecily screeched when they got back to her, "Oh why did you let him waste his money, Joseph? What were you thinking of? Honestly!" she tutted.

"Look, it's his money and he seems to know exactly what it's all for," Joseph shrugged.

Donkey's cart was piled high. So was Jenny's, with everything Joseph had bought earlier. When Nisa's dad came back he stood there, scratching his head for a minute.

"I'm going to have to charge you two for carting this lot back. A bag of extra carrots for the donkeys at least," he teased them as they set off home.

They wanted to get going early to avoid the queues for the ferry crossing, which Joseph offered to pay for. Despite their heavy loads, the donkeys still travelled faster than anyone on foot and they managed to catch the second river crossing that afternoon, after only a short wait.

"I'll have to charge you extra though, for carrying so much weight," the boatman told them, "Can't take as many people across, if there's carts and donkeys on board, see?"

"Talk to him," Nisa's dad replied, nodding at Joseph, "He's paying!" he laughed out loud.

Back at the village, Nisa had to wait a long time for the dragleon. Alice waited with her, wanting to come along too, which was nice. It seemed like ages before they finally heard her calling from the edge of the village, which was odd. It turned out that she didn't want to worry people by walking through the streets. She wasn't sure how welcome she'd be, after last time.

The three of them set off holding hands, with Jasmine in the middle, idly swinging their arms back and forth. She didn't want to go far, saying that she had one of her funny feelings. So they agreed to go to the lake again, but through the forest on that side of the village, for a change.

Nisa wondered if her funny feeling might have something to do with water lilies, possibly?

It was all a bit of a mess, not being one of Jasmine's usual haunts. The trails were so overgrown they were difficult to make out, in places. Jasmine didn't dare prune anything either, for fear it would only grow back twice as thick. The girls pushed back what they could, while she kicked and rolled the odd fallen tree trunk off the path. Dizzy mice and beetles spilled out of them and beat a hasty retreat into the undergrowth, which made the girls laugh.

It was heavy going for the dragleon, who had to force her way through everything, while Nisa and Alice could scamper under any tangled branches, or slip between the overgrown bushes. They all felt relieved when it opened up at last and their little lake came into view, not far ahead. Jasmine's tummy began to rumble at the thought of all those water lilies, just waiting to be eaten.

"We're going to have to tie you to one of Nathi's fishing lines, aren't we?" Alice reckoned.

"I beg your pardon, whatever for?" Jasmine wanted to know.

"So you don't float up, up and away like a big, bloated

balloon!" she squealed and ran away.

"Yeah, then we'll throw things at you and pop you!" Nisa shrieked and ran after Alice.

Jasmine lifted her nose in the air and waded into the lake, working out a way to get them both back, at once! The hippos merely moved out of her way, quite used to her by now. She began munching on the water lilies, relishing every mouthful as the fleshy leaves popped on her tongue and the inside of her cheeks. It tickled, along with all the fish that nibbled at her scales.

"Jasmine? Did you hear what the boatman said to Nathi the other day?" Nisa called over.

"No. What was that? Sorry, you'll have to come closer because I can hardly hear you."

"She must've heard you, or she wouldn't have known to say "No," Alice warned her in a whisper. Which Jasmine also heard, having such good hearing.

"He told him not to eat the plants that grow on this here lake," Nisa said, inching closer.

"He said what? Speak up!" the dragleon said, a little too loudly, "Ooh hoo hoo, tickles."

"HE SAID not to eat these water lilies, because once you start, you can't stop."

"Mmm. He's right there. Hee hee! I can't seem to get enough of them. They're delicious!"

"See. She heard that alright," Alice warned, but followed Nisa all the same.

"They're not just water lilies. He warned Nathi about them. What was it he called them? Lo' lotus something or other. Lotus leaves, or flowers, or lilies," Nisa recalled, inching closer still.

"I don't mind what they're called, when they taste this good, but you'll have to speak up or come closer, because I

188

can hardly hear you. Ooh hoo hoo hee hee!" the dragleon lied.

"She can, you know," Alice urged, but still edged closer with Nisa.

"He said there's a "leg's end" about them, but flowers don't have legs. Even I know that much. So maybe he was just pulling Nathi's leg? I don't know," Nisa admitted.

Jasmine had to try very hard not to chuckle at that, stuffing more of the lotus leaves into her mouth, to stop herself from laughing. Any excuse!

"Maybe it's more because of the air in them, you know, giving you wind," Alice suggested.

SPLASH! The dragleon whipped her long tail around in the water, drenching them both.

"Jasmine!" Alice squealed at her, suddenly dripping wet.

"Oh, YOU!" Nisa yelled, standing there soaking wet, with her arms outstretched.

They'd come close enough and the dragleon had got them both back, alright! She burst out laughing, sputtering bits of lily and leaf and causing the lotus flowers to burst into bloom all over again, all around her, replacing the very flowers she'd just eaten. Grinning, she began to pluck them straight away, stuffing the new flowers into her mouth as well.

"I think he meant a "legend." It means a tale from a long time ago, which people used to think was a true story. Did you hear that?" she said suddenly, sitting bolt upright and looking around.

"We're not falling for any more of your tricks," Nisa sneered, wringing her dress out.

"Yeah. Funny's funny, but enough's enough, okay?" Alice informed her, still dripping wet.

"No, really! I mean it. I heard it. I felt it. *Something*," Jasmine looked deadly serious. Either she was very good at acting, or something was definitely the matter.

189

The girls complained bitterly about having to leave, but Jasmine insisted they must. She didn't say why. She didn't know why, just that something had happened. She didn't know what.

High up in the hills a massive landslide had blocked, long ago, one end of a valley. It formed a dam, trapping water, which gave rise to a lake that spread back up the valley, getting deeper and wider over countless years. The river began up there as a waterfall, cascading down one side of the ancient rock fall, with grasses, ferns, bushes and trees growing right across the top of it, either side of the pretty stream that drained the lake, until now. After such heavy rains, the lake was so swollen that the little stream could no longer cope.

BOOOOOOOOOOOOOM!

The ancient rock fall suddenly gave way, crashing down in a mountain of spray that splashed right up the valley walls. The whole lake burst forth in a foaming torrent of white water. Vultures were dashed off the cliffs, goats swept off their feet. Homes were smashed to smithereens, trees ripped up by their roots and hurled on down the valley. It thundered along like a tidal wave, rolling boulders along the valley floor like marbles. Once it broke free of the hills, the teeming water surged on down the river, which instantly burst its banks.

Nathi and the grown-ups were back in the village by the time it struck, while Jasmine and the girls were hurrying back through the forest, when it hit.

Chapter Fifteen

A flash flood surged along the course of the river, crashing into the bends where it toppled the banks. Slabs of earth landed with great splashes, soil and stones washed away downstream.

A wall of water raced towards the ferry crossing, spilling over and soaking the plains. It thundered along, ripping out trees and bulldozing termite mounds, sweeping all before it the bodies of animals, bushes, whole tree trunks turning and snapping branches.

The crocodiles sensed the coming flood and crawled up into their holes, dug deep into the river banks. Turtles frantically buried themselves, deep and deeper down, into the mud. Birds took flight all along the river, while frogs hopped out and onto dry land, hoping for the best.

The ferry was tied to the shore, taking passengers on board when they all heard the noise. Everyone stood up on tip-toe or craned their necks, to see what it could be.

A great wash of water smashed around a bend in the river, bearing down on them all.

People turned to race back along the jetty, or followed the gazelle and wildebeest, sprinting for their lives across the plains. There was no time for those already on the boat.

"Hang on! Hold on tight!" the boatman shouted above the roar, "Brace yourselves!"

As the wave struck it lifted the boat up, hurling it forwards. The ropes snapped taught with a jolt. For a while they surfed on the crest of a wave, weaving on the rushing waters as the flood poured past, pulling at the ferry, splashing spray up over the sides.

Bushes and branches, rafts of turf, whole trees, dead

animals, even a thatched roof all hurtled past them, narrowly missing the boat.

People scattered across the plains. The spreading floodwater surged after them, gaining ground and catching them up, one by one, knocking them flat and flushing them far away.

The jetty crumpled in the torrent beside the boat, its splintered timbers dashed away.

A great baobab tree sailed by, spinning slowly on the rushing river.

The flash flood thundered away downstream, leaving the ferry behind, fighting the current, still tight on its ropes in a raging river.

A dead hippo swirled towards them, bloated and floating, upside down. It smacked into the boat with a dreadful jolt and burst open, in a sudden spray of stench. Someone screamed as the ropes snapped, flinging people overboard.

The ferry lurched after them, instantly sucked up by the swift current and swept away.

The floating baobab slammed into a bend, spearing the bank with stout branches. The whole tree stuck fast, its thick trunk buffeted by the flood. Other trees surged into it, sliding beneath in the slick waters, or locking branches to hold on, forming a giant snag.

The boat rose and dipped horribly, wildly adrift on the swollen river.

A racing tree edged towards them. Branches scraped down one side. As it barged past, pushing them aside, one of the branches snapped! Everyone screamed at the jarring jolt. The ferry rolled right over, hitting the water with a giant SLAP, throwing everyone overboard.

The flood swept them along, slipping underwater and bobbing back up again, gasping for breath between cries for help, one arm raised above their heads.

The dragleon heard their screaming. She burst out into the open, charging off towards the river.

"Go home!" she shouted, over her shoulder at the frightened girls.

In a fountain of spray, the ferry thumped into the snag. The heaving waters pushed it hard, forcing it under the baobab trunk. It sank with a giant GLOOP! Before welling back up in a rush of water on the other side, and spinning off downstream.

As people washed up to the snag, they reached out and clung on for dear life, hooking their elbows over its branches, grabbing at bunches of flimsy twigs. Stranded and gasping for breath, they spluttered in eddies of churning water, their legs swept out from under them.

As their arms, their elbows, hands and fingers all began to ache, the flood began to ease off, slowly but surely, slowing down. Its waters no longer roared, rampaging, wracking their bedraggled bodies, but sweeping by sullenly, swirling all around them.

People began to cry out, in pain and fear and concern for one another. Some risked splashing their way along the snag; husbands hoping to help their wives, people struggling to reach their neighbours, grown-ups doggedly splashing through the water, hoping to comfort crying children.

Splashing was the signal that the crocodiles had all been waiting for. They slithered out from their holes in the banks, hoping for the spoils.

The ground shook as the dragleon thundered across the plain. Splashing into the flood between two great walls of spray; she surged forwards, knee deep, tummy deep, water sloshing over her sides, pushing on towards the sound of people, crying out for help.

As the land fell away beneath her front feet, she pushed off with her hind legs, diving into the river with one almighty splash! She came up swimming hard, weaving through the water like a giant, fat snake. She reached the baobab roots, sticking up out of the river, hauling herself along them to pick up the first of the flood victims. A frightened woman threw herself at her, wrapping her arms around the base of her neck. Jasmine pulled herself further along, using the roots. A man threw his terrified son onto her back and launched at her himself, grabbing the base of her tail.

The girls joined the rest of the villagers, where they stood in silence. They gazed out across a sea of standing water, with the river out there somewhere, coursing through the middle of it all. Some stood ankle deep while some began wading out, to see if they could help. Parents grabbed their children by the shoulders, to stop them following, no matter what.

Nisa found her dad and slipped her hand into his. Alice found her mum, who started crying.

Jasmine worked her way across the snag. More people clambered on board. They held onto her neck, her arms, her legs and tail, weighing her down in the water. She grappled along the smooth baobab trunk, digging her talons in, covered in people, all clinging on.

Somebody noticed the crocodiles fighting the current, fighting their way towards them!

A terrible scream passed from one person to the next. Frantic, they began to scrabble along the snag themselves. In amongst tree roots, over slippery branches, along the rounded baobab trunk with next to nothing to hold on to, desperate to get clear of the water, get out of the river, to get away. Because anything was better than crocodiles!

With a quick yelp, one woman went, slipping under the smooth trunk and out the other side. She was never seen again, but coming from the far side, everyone heard the watery clop of heavy jaws, as the crocodiles claimed their first victim. They panicked, all of them, struggling madly while Jasmine struggled madly to reach them, along with the river's crocodiles.

The dragleon worked her way along, picking up even more people.

They were getting heavier though, clinging to each other, spreading out around her, kicking against the water, buffeted by the swirling river, dragging her down, as the crocodiles closed in.

Jasmine began gasping for breath, her claws gouging grooves in the great baobab trunk. Its roots began to writhe, as if in pain. Her talons ached. Her arms ached. She could barely breathe, barely swim, barely even move.

The crocodiles bore down on them. Soon they'd be snapping around the edges and picking people off, one by one, dragging them down into the depths, to drown.

Try as she might, Jasmine realised she would never reach the shore in time, or even those that were left, screaming at her. Not before the crocodiles. Not with all these people in tow.

The villagers realised it too, trying to clamber over each other, on top of her; anything to get up out of the water, away from the edges, away from the crocodiles. They tugged on her ears, pulled at her wings, pulling her down and pushing her under, even clambering over her head.

The crocodiles sank beneath the surface, one by one, with scarcely a ripple.

To everyone's horror, the dragleon stopped struggling along! She stopped moving! Instead she bobbed upright in the river, gasping for breath, treading water, winded and trying to think.

"That's it! Winded! I can't hardly breathe. They're all

underwater now anyway, so it wouldn't help if I did, but maybe?" Jasmine's mind raced as she fought to cling on, "It stops the fish biting. I know that much. Did I eat enough? I must have, but will it work at all?" she wondered. There was nothing else for it though. She had to give it a try.

She forced herself to concentrate, to think of happier times. She closed her eyes, tensing her tummy muscles, bearing down, holding her breath and treading water. It felt like doing a jig, only underwater, like dancing through the streets with everyone! Happy as happy can be! Her cheeks bulged. Her neck bent round and down to one side. Her tummy gurgled horribly. She went purple, pushing down, cross-eyed with sheer effort, straining, almost bent double in the water, scrunching up her face, heaving down, muscles clenched, willing her own innards to please, JUST . . .

As the leading crocodiles chose their victims, the dragleon looked fit to explode!

. . . FAAAART! It was the greatest, loudest, longest fart in the history of the WORLD!

It foghorned out of her, thankfully underwater, bursting forth in scented jets of bubbles, which glooped together and wobbled upwards, blasting the on-coming crocodiles, full in their faces.

People were screaming and struggling still, when Jasmine's monstrous fart broke on the surface of the river. The air gurgled in a great cascade of bursting bubbles.

She waited with baited breath, to see if it had worked. People stopped screaming and struggling. One by one, they turned around in stunned silence.

"Did she just?"

"Uh-huh. She's been on them lotus lilies again, haven't you, miss?" gasped the boatman.

No attack came. Nobody went under. Not yet. Everyone

waited with baited breath.

"Ooh, what a lovely smell!" somebody noticed.

Jasmine strained and heaved some more, producing a second, truly thunderous fart. They all heard it. Bubbling up from the depths before it, too, burst fragrantly on the surface of the river.

"Blimey!" somebody said, as Jasmine finally found out what it did to the fish.

A perfect circle of smaller bubbles trickled up to pop delicately on the water's surface. A ring of sculling crocodiles followed, circling on their backs! They all clopped their jaws together and nose-dived like dabbling ducks, until only their tails stuck up out of the water. They waved them back and forth, flicking water everywhere, before dropping back down into the depths, as one.

People gasped as twenty crocodiles burst up from the river in a fountain of spray, all of them spinning around gracefully and daintily fluttering their eyelids. They were dancing! And waving! They flopped over onto their backs, sculling their webbed feet and swimming upside-down in a circle. They rolled over and over on the surface of the river and turned to face inwards like the spokes of a great wheel, which somehow spun round slowly.

In a cascade of falling water, the biggest crocodile of all burst up through the centre of the wheel, spinning a turtle on the end of his snout! It didn't look happy about it, without so much as a toe peeping out of its shell, while the crocodile seemed delighted with himself. He was grinning! They all were! Smiling like their leathery lives depended on it.

To everyone's astonishment, even Jasmine's, the crocodiles were synchronised swimming!

As the biggest crocodile sank back down, the others peeled away, somersaulting sideways into the river. They came up again shortly, bouncing the poor turtle from one to the next. Its little legs flailed in and out of its shell as they spun it through the air. You could hear it landing with a clop on one hard snout and then the next, before they all disappeared underwater again.

"Come on everyone. Never mind the show. Let's get you onto the bank, before whatever I've done to them wears off. I doubt they're going to be too happy about it," Jasmine warned.

The crocodiles swam in a figure of eight, which split into two figures of eight, perfectly timed to miss each other, as they gracefully swam through the centre.

"Ooh, look. It's like a giant flower!" Somebody said, while the rest of them craned their necks to watch. Quite how they managed to miss each other like that, was beyond everyone.

The hapless turtle clung on, looking shell-shocked, splay-legged across a crocodile's back. Never in its long life had it ever expected such abuse, which only got worse, before it got better.

The crocodiles continued to roll and dance and frolic out on the river, fluttering their eyelids and flicking the poor turtle from one to another, catching it in their jaws now.

They bobbed up and down and half turned, waving every so often, peeling off and out of their circle, one after the other and sometimes all at once, still smiling their scary, fixed smiles.

The dragleon scrabbled at soil and sodden turf. She'd reached the bank at last, slopping up out of the river and dragging everyone to safety with her. They all turned to watch, flabbergasted, intrigued, as the crocodiles continued their elegant display of synchronised swimming.

The villagers rushed forwards to help, splashing through the floodwater that covered the plains.

Ankle deep, knee deep and almost up to their waists as

they got nearer the river. Mouths dropped open when they saw what was happening. Everyone stared out over the water.

The crocodiles carried on without a care in the world, grinning and swimming in formation, quite beautifully. They twirled and dived and sunk and swam and splashed and bobbed and flurried and flounced, all in perfect timing, fluttering their eyelids and waving, for all the world to see.

They looked graceful as never before and never again either, as their timing began to slip. Some of them stopped dancing and swimming and broke formation, looking a bit disgruntled.

The poor turtle took his cue, plopping off into the water and making good his escape.

"I think we'd better get out of this deeper water now," the dragleon pointed out.

The whole village backed up slowly, away from the river, step by step, fascinated. Nobody wanted to turn around, to stop watching the amazing river dance that was taking place, right in front of them. People shook their heads and smiled in wonder, scarcely able to believe it.

The crocodiles could scarcely believe it either, as their synchronised swimming broke up, once and for all. They stopped grinning and looked confused instead, eying each other suspiciously, wondering if they'd really just done that and why? He did. I saw him. And her! But did I?

A warm little hand wormed its way into the dragleon's wet talons. She looked down to see Nisa standing beside her, looking back up at her.

"Thank goodness you're alright. I was worried about you, for a moment," Nisa admitted.

Jasmine scooped her up and hugged her, before turning her back on the river and sploshing on up to the village, where Nathi sat waiting for them all.

Everyone gathered round, making a huge fuss of the survivors and working out who'd gone, or been flushed away across the plains. They were probably still alive, if somewhat bedraggled.

"I'll cross over and fetch them back tomorrow, those I can find. I'm too done in right now."

"Jasmine, I sometimes wonder how we ever managed without you," one of the elders said.

"Probably a whole lot better," she cocked her head and thought for a moment, "But with less entertainment, I fancy," she replied, managing a chuckle, despite feeling utterly exhausted.

"THREE CHEERS FOR JASMINE, everybody!" he shouted out.

"Oh no, please. Honestly, there's no need for that," she wasted her breath and went pink.

"Hip, hip . . ." he led the cheers, "HOORAY!" the whole village cheered. Three times.

After that display, the crocodiles had surely earned a place in the next Dragleon Festival. At least the costumes should be a doddle, compared to the ants with all their fiddly legs and feelers.

Chapter Sixteen

The long dry season got underway, after disappointing rains. In the wake of the flood though, it took fully two weeks before the plains began to dry out.

Outside school, Nathi spent every spare minute he had, hammering and scraping and sawing things in his little workshop. He flatly refused to tell anyone what he was up to, except his parrot, which sat on his shoulder whenever it could. It soon learned that was probably the safest place to be in there, after nearly being knocked off its perch by a bouncing hammer.

Nisa spent much of her spare time with Jasmine and Alice, out in the woods. They played hide and seek or dragleon's footsteps, marvelling at the flowers that popped up all around her.

"Why don't we go to the lake again tomorrow? You could eat some of those lotus lilies you love so much," Nisa asked Jasmine, while they relaxed among her flowers after a game of tag.

"Oh, I'd love to, but the more of those lilies I eat, the more I want to eat. I can't seem to get enough of them, which can't be right, can it? I've been thinking about eating them all the time lately and I'm just not having it. I didn't even notice either, until you mentioned the boatman warning Nathi about them," Jasmine admitted, drooling despite herself.

"I'm sure Nathi will be pleased to hear it, on the whole. Every time you *farted* underwater, the fish stopped biting. They must've been too busy swimming and dancing, like the crocodiles did."

"It was so funny though, when Nathi got all cross with

201

you," Alice sniggered.

"I bet they looked lovely down there, if only we'd been able to see it," Jasmine chuckled.

Other children often joined in with their games in the woods. Whenever there were enough of them, they had some new games too now, sometimes 'copying crocodiles' by dancing around in circles, rolling and waving and smiling and bobbing and turning in formation, only without the water. It rather worried the local tortoises, since turtles and tortoises speak a very similar language and they'd all heard what happened down at the river. Sometimes the children played 'anty antics' where they line danced around the forest, hopelessly out of time, stomping, stepping, linking arms and turning, shuffling, clapping their hands and of course their very favourite move; wiggle those little ant bottoms! The children absolutely loved it, happy as happy can be, dancing with the dragleon, in forests full of flowers.

Their parents knew they'd be perfectly safe, with Jasmine watching over them like a giant mother hen. She always brought them back to the village, safe and sound. These days they could even feel them coming home, thanks to another of their new games. The children called it the 'dragleon dance,' much to Jasmine's delight. They insisted that she go first, always, like she did with the grown-ups when they danced through the streets. The ground shook for miles around, each time the dragleon led a long line of cheerful children, dancing a ragged conga. Kicking and hopping and swaying from one side to the other, while walloping back home across the village clearing, laughing and kicking up flowers as they went. They'd soon grow back again anyway.

Whenever they could, their parents thanked her by feeding her doughnuts on the village clearing, which of course Jasmine loved. With each and every doughnut she ate, more flowers sprang up beside her. Before long they had to be careful where they fed her, for fear of blocking the roads with yet more of her flowers. You couldn't see where you were driving and they snagged terribly, if too many got caught up in the cart wheels.

One fine day, the elders went down to inspect the plains and fields with the village farmers. They poked and prodded and put all their weight on the rich soils, testing them. Having soaked up so much water, the ground looked as good as ever for planting this year's crops.

While most of the grown-ups eagerly awaited their return, most of the children were dreading it. Sure enough though, it was time to start planting again. The news gained the children a break from school, but gained them weeks of work in the fields instead.

Soon after that, the hard work began in earnest. The fields and plains needed preparing, before anything could be planted. The soil was wet and heavy and ploughing it into furrows proved a back-breaking task which went on, and on, and on.

Nisa's father came home each evening and flopped down into his chair, exhausted.

Even the donkeys slept lying down in their stables, where normally they stood up. Nisa did her best to spoil them both, with lots of carrots and fusses, but she was tired out herself. While the men ploughed the ground, the children followed on behind, weeding it. Carefully, since the donkeys sometimes left dollops of fertiliser in their wake!

Most of the womenfolk sorted out the storage sheds, deciding what to use for food, what to sell at markets and what to use for planting this year's crop.

Jasmine all but disappeared, planting and primping her new patch of forest. Weeding was not one of her strong points, since every plant she touched grew back twice as fast and twice as big as before. Tilling the soil was just as bad, if she sliced through any roots.

Nathi did one of two things, mostly. Either clanking and hammering and sawing away in his shed at all the bits and bobs he'd bought at the big market, or fishing on the little lake. He couldn't go alone though and only one grown-up had any free time on their hands. Thankfully, he was only too happy to go along and keep an eye on him.

"It's either that or twiddle me thumbs, waiting for me new boat to arrive. I wish they'd hurry up with it an' all. It all adds up, yer small change and I don't like missing out," he grinned, holding up a bag of coins, "I held onto this for dear life, I did. Tied fast to me belt it was, whilst we was wildly adrift on the river. Good job I did an' all though, eh?"

"I'll say. Nobody's been able to cross the river since, except those Jasmine carried over, the day after. But those crocodiles must've been a sight for sore eyes. Pity I couldn't see it."

"There was nearly some very rich crocodiles that day though," the boatman shuddered.

"Oh I'm sorry. I didn't think. I didn't mean to be rude."

"No, not at all, but if it hadn't been for Jasmine, I reckon I'd have ended up in a fair few crocodile bellies. Never mind this little lot," he lifted his purse again, smiling.

Nathi went out on the lake, to earn some small change of his own with each and every fish he caught. Except a couple for the boatman, a couple for his mum and a couple for Nisa's mum, too.

The dragleon returned once planting got underway. Along with everyone else, she worked tirelessly from dawn 'til dusk. After helping Nisa and her dad all morning, she'd help as many other people as she could to get their crops out, sowing this or digging in that. Whatever she touched would grow quicker and stronger than anything else around. So it looked like they'd all be in for another bumper harvest this year, or possibly even two, in places.

The donkeys were glad of the rest, after all their hard work tilling the soil.

They enjoyed a peaceful fortnight or so, but as soon as the planting was done, they were put to work once more. Whatever was left over went to market and it was the donkey's job to cart it there. At least the roads were free of mud by now, which made the going much easier.

Nisa's parents were in dire need of a rest themselves, but knew this one last thing just had to be done. There was something Nathi wanted to do too, apart from selling his fish. So they took him along, with Joseph and Cecily to watch over him. They could all rest afterwards.

Nathi finally revealed what he'd been up to with all those bits of junk, when he proudly dragged a second wheelchair out of his shed, which he'd made all by himself, from scratch!

"All that hard work for someone else, with no hope of payment," Cecily shook her head.

There was something under a blanket too, resting across his lap. They couldn't make it out, but it seemed to have a shoe stuck on one end of it, of all things! The other of the pair sat on his lap.

"I'm more proud of this, to be honest," Nathi admitted, "If it works anyway. I think it should."

He pulled it out from under the blanket, lifting up what looked like a false leg. It even had a bendy joint where the knee would be and another, slightly less bendy, for an ankle.

"What on earth is that thing for?" Cecily screeched, having never seen a false leg before.

"Not so much what, as whom?" Nisa's mum realised, "Those children at the market. Yes?"

As soon as she saw that wheelchair and the false leg he'd

made, Nisa pretty much knew what Nathi had wished for: to help those children less fortunate than himself. Her hand slipped gently into her mother's because she'd worked it out too, more or less. Nisa could tell.

Joseph bent down to look at the workmanship, slowly shaking his head in disbelief.

"Sheesh, son. This is amazing! The attention to detail, the metalwork, all the joints, the strap work and padding. I've never seen anything like it," he gasped, turning it over in his hands.

"I think the chief difficulty will be the added strain on her lumbar vertebrae and gluteus maximus and medius muscles on the false limb side, because of course they'll have withered after such a prolonged period of effective dormancy," Nathi explained, completely baffling them all.

"You see, she'll need to develop a rather swivelling gait, for which the posterior leg muscles will be essential. That and the chafing of course, where the prosthetic adjoins her upper thigh."

"Eh?" they didn't see, "Is he speaking another language, d'you think?"

"Um. Only half her bum works now, but she'll need to grow the muscles of the other half back to use the false leg. Oh and it'll give her back ache and rub a bit, at first," Nathi translated.

Nisa chuckled, having heard all this sort of thing before, in class.

"We don't use words like "bum", Nathi," Cecily objected, at which Nisa burst out laughing.

"Okay, sorry. Gluteus maximus then, like I said in the first place," he said with a shrug.

"Oh pardon me for being your mother and minding your manners, I'm sure," Cecily snorted.

"I think I've got it covered, provided she builds usage up gradually, strengthening the rectus femoris and both abductor muscle groups, which I'm pretty sure will still be attached to her femur, unlike her vastus lateralis and mederalis, which can't be, at least not by their anterior ligaments."

"He's off again," Nisa's dad scratched his head.

"I made sure the joints on the prosthetic are definitely load-bearing and all materials are lightweight and hard-wearing, which is of course essential for sustained usage of the prosthetic, as a consistent means of locomotion," he explained, with just a hint of concern in his voice.

"Huh?" Joseph looked at Cecily, wondering where all this gobbledygook had come from.

A smile crept slowly across his face. He began to nod knowingly as it dawned on him too; it must be something to do with whatever his son had wished for.

"I see what Gloria was on about now," Cecily's mouth carried on opening and closing for a while, even after she'd finished speaking.

"Some muscles will still be attached to what's left of her thigh bone, but some won't, which will probably have shrivelled. I think it should take her weight. Oh and I made it tough."

"Shall we just get them with us to market, so they can try them out?" Nisa's dad suggested.

"If they're still there? They might not be," Nathi worried.

Nisa begged them to let her come too, but her dad flatly refused this time. Folding his arms and sticking his chin out, he said that she might put some silly people off buying from them. As if he wouldn't! It wasn't fair. She went back to her room in a sulk and sat down heavily, watching the remaining mantis baby catch a teeny weeny fly.

The others had all left, leaving just this one behind to

watch over her. It liked to sit on her new shelf, riding on her carved wooden animals, as if taking its rightful place amongst her most treasured things, including a thorn needle and an ostrich egg, with holes in them.

Nathi kept his eyes peeled all morning. Customers kept getting in his way. He kept craning his neck around them, hoping to spot the children through the crowds.

"Young man! Do you want to sell me some fish, or not?" one woman snapped at him.

"Oh. Sorry, Madam. I was keeping an eye out for two children. Neither of them can walk and I made them . . . something. It's important. Do you know who I mean? Have you seen them?"

"My husband's dinner is more important to me, but yes, I think I know who you mean. They're around here somewhere. Not that I took much notice and neither should you, if you ask me."

Instead he asked her if she could tell them that he wanted to see them, if she saw them again.

"Certainly not! I wouldn't want to encourage them," she answered and left in a huff.

"I would," Nathi said as she bustled off in her costly sandals, which flapped beneath her heels.

"Don't worry. They'll turn up soon enough," Nisa's mum tried to reassure him.

Sure enough, soon enough, there they were! Shuffling and hobbling along the edge of the crowd, the two children made their way towards him. The young girl risked an unsteady wave in all the hustle and bustle. Both of them seemed happy to see him, chatting away like Lord and Lady Muck, which made all three of them giggle, until Cecily brought the wheelchair and the false leg out from under the stall.

The look on their faces made all his hard work worthwhile, as far as Nathi was concerned.

They simply could not believe it, what he'd made for them, for nothing! He said so.

The little boy gleefully scrabbled up into his new chair, turning around to face the world like a new King, seated on his throne for the very first time.

The girl needed help understanding the straps that attached the false leg to her stump and waist. She sat down whilst Cecily helped her, following Nathi's careful instructions.

"It's quite easy, when you know how," she decided, putting the other brand new shoe on her own foot and shouting, "IT FITS!" for everyone to hear.

At first she pushed up with her hands, wobbling unsteadily, but slowly and carefully she managed to raise herself, until she was standing up. Actually standing up! She could scarcely believe it, without a stick, on her own two feet!

"But one of them's not really your foot, is it?" the little boy risked pointing out.

"Well I own them both, don't I? On my own two shoes then!" she told her annoying friend.

Looking up, the young girl stretched both her arms up to the blue sky, as if trying to reach out and touch it for the very first time. It seemed such a simple thing, to reach for the sky. Yet Nathi realised that she'd never been able to do it before, without letting go of her crutch.

The little boy was off!

"Mind yer backs! Coming through!" he shouted, wheeling around people with a great big grin on his face. It was a joy to watch. Never had anyone seen a child so happy.

For the girl, it took longer to take her first, unsteady steps. Joseph and Cecily walked either side of her, supporting her by the elbows. She did it though, putting one foot in front of the other, one at a time. Perhaps even more importantly, she carried on doing it, even after they'd both let go.

"I'm walking, I'm walking! On my own! Look!" she almost screamed at her little friend, as he zoomed past in his new chair, still grinning.

She wobbled, and very nearly fell over, but managed to steady herself and carry on. She changed direction, slowly and again, more sharply. She soon got quicker and more confident at walking, until she turned right around to face them, spinning on her new false leg.

The look on her face was magical, every bit as magical, as the wish that had made it possible.

Meanwhile Jasmine basked in the warm sunshine with Nisa resting against her, telling her what Nathi had made and was doing right now and why she wasn't allowed to go, or she would have.

"I don't suppose having me around would help much either. I'd probably clear the whole market!" Jasmine joked, "Besides, it's nice enough here on the edge of my woods, isn't it?"

"I guess so, amongst all your beautiful flowers. It's so unfair though, when me and you helped him more than anyone, with his fishing and making a wish and everything," Nisa grumbled.

"He doesn't need our help with fishing any more though, does he? I'm glad too because I mean to steer clear of that lake for a while, with all its wretched lotus lilies."

Nisa managed a smile at that, watching a butterfly flutter by. A chameleon had been watching it too, hidden amongst the flowers, which it settled on. Nisa squeaked as usual, when its long tongue shot out and grabbed the butterfly by the head, hauling it back to its chomping jaws.

"You little monster! I wish you lot wouldn't do that," she scoffed, but quickly forgave it.

The dragleon smiled, thinking that she wasn't the only one who talked to chameleons.

"Jasmine? Do you know, I mean, I know it tires you out and everything, but could someone make a second wish, after the first one they made? Say, if what they wanted had changed?"

"It wouldn't feel right somehow. Nope," the dragleon decided, "It doesn't, so I suppose not. Who were you thinking of?" she asked, knowing full well who Nisa was thinking of.

"Only, when I made my wish, it was only for me and it wouldn't be now, I don't think."

"When you made your wish, you had a great deal on your mind. Besides, you and so many other people are so much happier since. Me included," the dragleon reminded her.

"It seems so small now though, almost selfish compared to Nathi's," Nisa worried.

"Yet somehow it's helping so many people all around you, including Nathi making his wish. Like the ostrich that helps all the other animals. Isn't that what you told me the Wise One said?"

"Yes I suppose. When you put it like that," Nisa thought aloud.

"Unless, hold on. Remind me. Other than something nice to eat, did you wish for anything when I made you those second berries? You remember, the bobbly ones that made your tongue go all purple? What was it you called them?" Jasmine prompted her.

"Blackberries! And no I don't think I did, you know?" Nisa sat up and half turned around.

"Well maybe, just maybe you understand, there's another wish out there somewhere, still waiting for you to make it?" Jasmine suggested, "If it works at all and if we can find it, because I can't remember where we made those blackberries. Can you?"

"No, but of course I'd like to try! Who wouldn't? Can we? Go and look for them? Please?"

"Yes. I don't see why not. What harm can it do? If they're still growing," the dragleon yawned, "But not today and not for a while either, because I'm plumb tuckered out, Nisa."

"Ooh, another adventure for another time then. I can hardly wait," Nisa's eyes sparkled. Her mind began to race with more and more questions about wishes.

"What about Mum? Dad? Joseph and Cecily? They know about making a wish now too."

"I think grown-ups have too much on their minds. All their thoughts get in the way of what they're really feeling, it seems to me. I doubt my magic could get past it all, to reach what's deep down in their heart of hearts," Jasmine reasoned, as the bushes behind them rustled and parted.

Something much bigger than scorpions and far more dangerous to children slunk out of the forest and slid his cheek along Jasmine, wafting his tail in the air. After head-butting Nisa, the leopard flopped down and rolled over onto his back, with all four paws in the air. Nisa idly stroked his tummy, as if it were a perfectly normal thing to do.

The dragleon stretched her neck out, resting her chin on the ground.

"There'll be other children at other markets and in other villages too, won't there? Nathi wished to help as many as he can. Didn't he?" Nisa turned her head, waiting for answers.

None came, but the dragleon had long since worked out Nathi's wish and right now, she couldn't think of anything nicer. A single sunflower sprouted beside her, pushing up to stand head and shoulders above all the other flowers.

"Such a nice boy," was all she said at last, closing her eyes.

And the sunflower burst into bloom, bright bold yellow, against the big blue sky.

THE END
(For now, at least)

Acknowledgements

I would like to take this opportunity to thank Sonia Land of Sheil Land Associates for her continued and invaluable patience, advice, support, criticism and encouragement and for recognising the dragleon's potential to become a series of books (at least).

I hope *Dancing With The Dragleon* is a quick-step in the right direction.

Thank you also to Gabrielle Hancock of Sheil Land Associates, for her technical support and patience, when dealing with my Neanderthal understanding of information technology.

Thank you so much to Jennifer Haydon for her unflinching belief in my debatable abilities, all her feedback and her infectious enthusiasm for the simple things in life, like Kew Gardens and snowdrops and soil and worms and chaffinches that tell you off, when it's past their tea time!

Tracy Davies has been a dear friend of mine for more years than either of us cares to count, but her encouragement and belief have meant a great deal to me since I began to write. She presumed and expected me to get there in the end and I wouldn't want to disappoint her. Mind, I still prefer Jersey cows and donkeys to Angora goats, even yours Tracy.

Talking of animals, I'd actually like to thank Bompa, my trusty Bullmastiff, who is probably affected by my writing more than anyone. Bless him for letting me get on with it for hours on end without ever nagging me when it's past his tea time, or his walk is overdue. Sometimes he does come up and demand a cuddle though, to which he's always welcome.

And talking of dogs I'd like to thank Jeanette Parfette

Jeanette of Walthamstow, as I call her) for being the
ɔst dog sitter anyone could possibly wish for and looking
after them all in my absence, over so many years. Without
her, I couldn't have done half of it, especially the travelling.

A hearty acknowledgement must go to Allister Thomas for
being a friend indeed, when I was a friend in need. Apologies
to him and all primary school teachers for the occasional
'THEN' slipping, albeit self consciously into the pages of this
book. I must try harder next time.

Well done to Jeffrey Peters for completing the London
Marathon and for complaining that he wasn't granted
enough words in the acknowledgements section of my first
published book, *The Dragleon*. Your good self and Esin are
always welcome to a few more kind words, in my book.

Thanks to Peter Slater, my one time Creative Writing
Tutor, who continues to take an interest and offers more than
welcome advice and criticism. I doubt I'd be writing this at
all, if it hadn't been for your superlative tuition in the first
place.

I'd like to mention Laura Salas-Ortiz for being her
wonderful self over the decades and my 'muse' when it comes
to writing about Nisa.

Thanks to Malcolm Rippeth for the watercolours and
agapanthus and just being a good mate.

And finally, because I think she'll be chuffed to bits to see
her name in print, when it should be up in lights if you ask
me; to Ivy Murray, for being a wonderful neighbour, for all
the laughs, all the treats for the dogs and all the practice with
modern technology, trying to work out her latest gadget or
gizmo.

About the Author

Guy Waddilove was born and raised and just about educated in the beautiful town of Ilkley in the Yorkshire Dales. He studied for a BSc Modular degree and later took a post-graduate diploma in Careers Guidance from the University of East London. After several years advising on employment, careers and confidence building, and when several close friends and family died in sadly rapid succession, he found what was really important in his life was to achieve some of his ambitions.

His passion in life was wildlife and the natural world, with a side order of ancient history, so he travelled the world extensively to witness many of the world's natural and man-made wonders and what was left of both. He finally decided to make himself useful to the conservation cause and volunteered as a Keeper in a well known zoo where he has now been with them for well over six years.

Printed in Great Britain
by Amazon.co.uk, Ltd.,
Marston Gate.